THE CORPSE PRIEST

CARSON WINTER

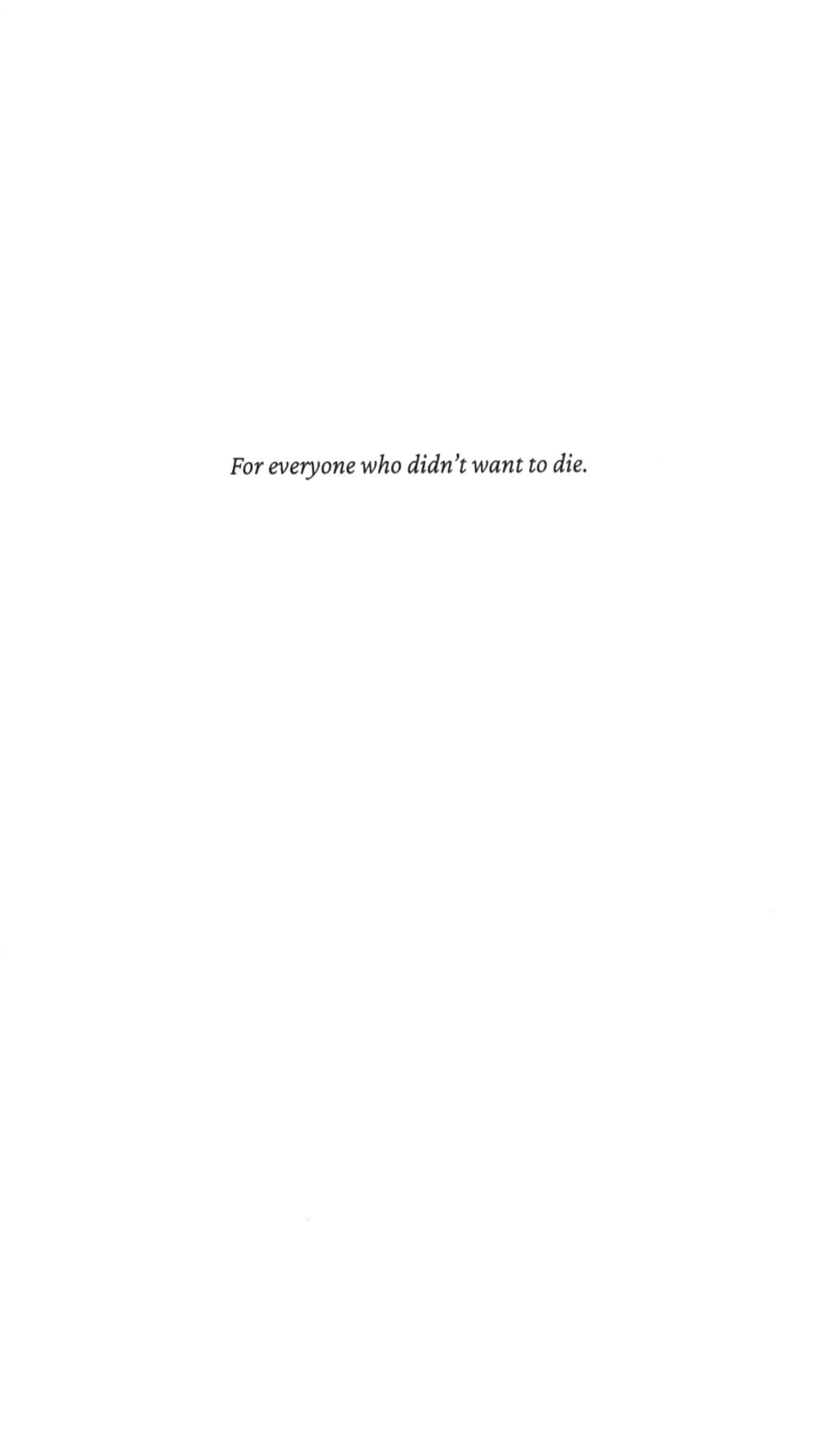

For everyone who didn't want to die.

1

CORPSE, WALKING

The city stood before him, towering and teeming. Populated or infested, he could not tell.

In its center stood a castle. In its shadow, a church—a parody of its gargantuan brother. Stone, with spires all its own—it wound its way like a serpent through the city, a building as long as a mile, twisting and turning through the sprawl. Its attendees came and went as they pleased, leaving their homes to worship, then returning to tend to their livestock, crops, or molten steel.

The stranger was tall, but not giant. Lean, but not skinny. His hair was shorn like that of a monk, a translucent prickling of black that barely masked a series of intricate tattoos on his skull. Under heavy eyebrows sat sullen eyes—deep seated and weary. His beard was thick and unkempt. His fingernails were black with dried blood. On his side hung a sword.

The stranger had only just entered the city when he felt people watching him. Across the street, a mother and her children stared, their mouths slightly agape.

He followed the lengthy church's serpentine body,

imagining it as a refuge, the spring from which this community flowed. The church was long and beautiful. In winter, it was no doubt packed with these sad, tired people —all of them bracing for some unknown hand to strike.

The stranger lingered by a fruit stand, eyeing jewels of magenta berries sold for next to nothing. He flipped the farmer a coin and leaned against a storefront, feeling the sweetness coat his tongue.

Down the dirt street, some small commotion erupted.

A guard and his riding cat stopped. The beast reared up and the armored man slid off its back, swishing his cape out of the way. A broadsword hung heavily at his hip.

The stranger narrowed his eyes.

There was a man there, playing music on a six stringed instrument, plucking out an admittedly grating melody.

The bard did not look up when the guard stood before him.

Obviously annoyed that his presence had not been perceived, the guard took another large step toward the bard, then reached out and grabbed the lute by its neck, tearing it from his hand.

The bard met his agitator's gaze. "Excuse me, sir," he said, with a heavy accent.

"You're disturbing the peace," said the guard.

"I am playing music."

"Music?" The guard turned slightly, as a showman, to see if the commoners would laugh with him. Instead, they stared at the earth. To the bard he said, "Where are you from?"

"The Ghostcliffs."

"I pity the state of the arts there."

With a giant hand, he reached out to grab the bard's head, his outstretched fingers holding him like a ball. With a taut snap of his arm, he threw the bard backwards into the muddy street.

The tattooed man let the rest of his berries drop. He squeezed between the shoulders of retreating commoners, a fish swimming upstream.

The bard rolled in the muck, his eyes covered in the thick earthen batter. He righted himself on his hands and knees, but before he could stand, the red-furred feline opened its fanged mouth and hissed. The bard froze.

"Good girl," said the guard, a wicked grin crossing his lips. He reached a tender hand to the horse-sized cat, scratching her chin. "I think Ingrit is hungry."

The guard advanced. His foot smashed through the lute's body. It cracked and splintered, the strings snapping violently.

"Not from around here, are you?"

"No, sir," said the bard. Then, he added, "But you know that."

"Do I?"

"I already told you. I'm from the Ghostcliffs."

"You think you're very clever then?"

The bard said nothing and the guard drew his sword.

The stranger approached quietly, his hand on his pommel—pushing through throngs of the brave or ill-minded that remained. He could barely hear the bard's silence ceasing, as his lips moved nearly imperceptibly in his own language.

The guard whistled to his cat and the great beast leapt lightly to her feet, its icy predator eyes glued to the mumbling bard.

"*Za't problimenk dakari.*"

The guard's blade sliced through the air, his face twisted in mad glee.

With some pity, the stranger recognized the bard—he was a man who did not want to die.

The stranger lunged forward; but as soon as he did, the guard's blade halted in mid-air.

One child dropped her flowers and ran screaming. The roar of the city fell silent, like the earth inside a grave.

The guard swung the point of his sword from bard to stranger.

"Another foreigner?" asked the guard.

The stranger did not speak. His muscles hardened under his skin, his fingers wrapped around his sword's grip.

"I saw your advance, you inked beast. Where are you from?" The guard closed in on the stranger, one brash foot in front of the other. "Tell me, hero—what were you going to do?"

The stranger said nothing.

"Deaf? Dumb?"

He shook his head slowly. The guard's point, despite his bluster, wavered in the air. He was untrained, sloppy. His grip weak, his form nonexistent.

"Do you wish to die?" asked the stranger, finally. It was not a threat, but an earnest question.

In his mind, he saw the action unfold in a breath. The guard would lift his blade and swing, horizontal along a sloping axis. The stranger would catch the blade with his own, pushing it down with his own strength, then thrust forward. One parry, one deep push, and the stranger's blade would rinse itself in the guard's insides.

The man on the ground screamed. "*DAKARI EST ULL!*"

The guard staggered, his blade's silver tip meeting the earth. He wore a curious expression on his face. Pain, terror —but most of all confusion. His arms stretched out in front of him.

The stranger remained still, his hand resting around his sword's grip.

The cat, Ingrit, purred impotently. Her pupils widened as she saw her master claw at his own face. With a fierce hiss, she turned and darted down the street to safety.

The guard pointed to the bard, trying to speak. But nothing came out.

Except one thing.

Blood.

Lots of it.

The bard stood tall, wiping the muck from his face as the guard gagged between hacking coughs and organs slipping out from between his teeth.

A crimson fountain rained out of his gaping maw, soaking his tunic. The villagers no longer seemed afraid, but curious. They relaxed, leaned on posts; some wore expressions of amusement as the guard thrashed wildly and vomited his stomach lining into the mud.

The stranger's ears perked up.

Down the road, galloping.

"You should go," he said to the bard.

The man looked down to his lute. For a moment, the stranger thought the bard would not leave. He watched him closely, unsure of what this meant for either of them. But as the sound of the guards grew louder, the bard took his advice quietly and turned away, disappearing down an alley. The stranger was right. The man did not want to die.

Meanwhile, the guard had fallen to his knees. His eyes had been sucked back into his skull, pulverized into jelly—now drooling out of his mouth as pink viscous fluid.

Another three came barreling down the street. When they found their comrade, they recoiled at his state.

"Fuck the Martyr!" yelled a man atop a cat.

"Loor! What happened to you, man?"

The guard, before he died, before his brain trickled down the back of his throat and out of his mouth, reached with a feeble arm—trembling as mightily as the tip of his blade. He pointed.

And these men, dressed in armor and wearing the finest weapons gold could buy, followed this finger, to find it pointing at a strange man with a black, scraggly beard and tattooed skull. Sullen and dreary by his very nature.

"You! There! What is your name?"

The name came off his lips like dirt from the grave. "Corpse," he said.

2

A BRIEF AND BLOODY BATTLE

THEY WERE MAYBE ten feet away, closing in, their formation that of a three-point noose, slowly tightening on the tattooed man.

Corpse said nothing. There was no warning to offer. The men had already chosen their end.

One rushed forward with his blade above his head, such that his whole body was exposed. Corpse dipped his blade in surprise.

These are not soldiers, he thought. A curious discomfort bubbled within him.

The guard ran straight toward him and Corpse only had to extend his blade to let it pierce through the gaps in the guard's armor, right into his shoulder. Blood spurted from the wound, and the sword dropped from the foolhardy guard's hands before he could swing. He jerked away from the flesh wound, keeling over in the street.

"Fuck!" he screamed. His arm hung loose as his other cradled the injured appendage.

The tip of Corpse's blade was red with blood.

The next two attacked him at once, but they too were

weak swordsmen. They swished their blades back and forth through the air for reasons Corpse could not discern. Surely this was the sort of tactic that would successfully deter an army of children, but not a single trained soldier.

Their blades swung like two out of time pendulums; Corpse waited for his time to strike. When one guard had his blade far across him, leaving his elbow open to an attack, Corpse gingerly sliced at the crook of his arm, cutting tendons and notching bone. The guard yelped and jumped back. His hand lost control of the blade. Meanwhile, the other guard, in complete shock, glanced to his comrade and, with a flushed, rageful face, lunged toward Corpse with hate in his eyes.

But the stranger circled his blade, locking it out, and pushed the tip of his own deep through the guard's arm.

Another cry.

Corpse pulled the blade from the man's body. Arterial blood spurted from the new wound.

They would live. The greatest cut was to their egos.

The first two went for their fallen swords, grasping them with their good arms.

"Please do not do this," pleaded Corpse.

But they did not heed his warning.

The commoners cowered in alleys, seeking safety from the violence. The humiliated guards tested their swords. Corpse sighed.

"GUARDSMEN OF DROSS TOLL!" one yelled. "COME!"

Distantly, Corpse heard the sound of galloping paws. *So, that was it. If they could not accept defeat, they would force their success. Very well.*

The guards approached, eager to taste his blood.

He sheathed his blade and turned away.

"Halt, stranger!"

Despite their order, they did not run toward him again. He passed commoners who backed away from him when he passed, but they said nothing, nor did they do anything, except smirk at the bloodied guards who now waited for their comrades.

Behind him, he heard the arrival of riding cats and fragments of the conversation that followed.

"Where'd he go?"

"Down that alley."

"And you let him go?"

"We—we were waiting."

"Fuck the Martyr."

He turned and twisted through the narrow passages of the city, wary of the shambling feet that followed only a couple turns behind him.

When he came to a clearing, he searched for a place to hide. He did not want to kill these men.

The winding body of the church stood in front of him, swallowing droves of people as they cascaded into its twisting form. Without a second thought, he dived into the crowd, vanishing. Behind him, six guards spilled out onto the street. Three of them bloodied with limp arms and wobbling swords.

But Corpse had become one of many. He pulled the hood of his cloak over his tattooed head and suddenly he was no one.

Inside the structure, Corpse continued to make distance, following its serpentine walls to make his way surreptitiously across the city, outside of the guards' purview. The people in the church began to find their seating.

He searched behind him in the thinning crowds. If the

guards had followed him into the church, he could not see them.

Corpse found a wooden pew and stared up at one of many pulpits, surrounded by a moon-sliver of torches. Every three hundred feet or so, there was a new pulpit, and in front of it a new audience. No priest stood before him now, but the stained glass windows told a tale through colored glass. A two-headed woman impaled on a stake, one face twisted in utter rage, the other in delight. She looked at him with her four sparkling eyes and Corpse could swear that they shimmered. Behind the two-headed woman, was a violet mountain that seemed to reach to the stars.

Beside him, he heard a voice. "You're a stranger."

His heart leapt. Corpse turned to see a woman, thrice his age with emerald-stained lips. "Yes," he said.

"Are you lost?"

His eyes shot to the church's opening. "No, I'm visiting."

He turned to his left and right, to see the hollows of the church stretch so far that he could not see their end. There were thousands inside, spread in pews that traveled in curves along with the shape of the church, breaking only for walkways. At the pulpit closest to him, a priest stood. Others, a hundred or so feet down in either direction, and more beyond, did the same.

The woman touched his leg and bowed her head, signaling him to do the same. On the pulpit the priest began to speak, but so did all the others. They spoke in unison, each priest's words joined together and it was not the voice of one but the voice of many. They said the exact same words with the exact same intonation—a wall of sharp syllables and sibilance in a language he could not understand.

Corpse's eyes darted around him to see that the woman and others were mouthing along with the words of the priest. There were no guards in sight. When the sermon ended, Corpse felt little of anything. But he bowed his head all the same.

"What was the priest reciting?" he asked.

"Our doctrine."

"A story?"

"Yes."

"Verbatim."

"Indeed." She paused, staring deep into his eyes. "Are you hungry?" she asked.

"Yes."

When she touched his arm, he recoiled. But the woman did not act offended. Instead, she waited, patiently, as if she were handling a wild animal. She said, softly, "Alright, come with me."

The woman wore a long burlap robe, chalk-etched with sigils. Corpse followed her out of the church, staying close. Every so often, she'd stop, turn, and wave him forward. "Come now," she said.

Corpse did as she asked.

She led him down a street to where a series of shops sold their wares. If she noticed him looking behind him every dozen paces, she made no comment. Down at the end was a two story building, a wooden sign hung on chains proclaiming it as the Drunken Prophet. The woman climbed up the steps and ushered Corpse to follow her. Inside, a fire blazed and the smell of stew filled his nostrils.

"Take a seat," she said. To the man tending the bar: "Garrt, get this fellow an ale, please. A bowl of stew also."

"Aye."

"You can call me Mirth, by the way."

"Corpse," he said.

A blemish of concern crossed the woman's face.

The other patrons of the bar stared at him. Under the weight of their gaze, he made it his business to observe the scratchings on the table. Soon, a dark beer in a tin stein appeared before him. He drank it, relishing the alcohol as it hit his bloodstream. Then too came the stew. He swallowed steaming chunks of beef, letting the brown juices drip down into his beard. When he finished the bowl, the woman served him another.

"Eat up," said Mirth. "You look like shit."

"Thank you," he muttered.

She sat down across from him, unhurried and warm. "Corpse is an odd name around these parts."

"Yes," he agreed.

"You're from the Malwoods, then?"

Corpse sat straighter. "You know it?"

"I run an inn. I see all sorts come through here."

"Others from the Malwoods have been here?"

"No," she admitted. "But I know them nonetheless. Are you fleeing?"

Corpse considered the question. He decided not to burden her with the truth. "No," he said.

"Of course."

"Really."

"It's not my business now, is it?"

He wiped the juices from his beard with his cloak. "What do I owe you for the food?"

"Nothing. I like to feed people. It's a kind thing to do."

Corpse opened his mouth to protest but it was obvious the woman named Mirth would not allow it. Instead, he asked, "What city is this?"

"Dross Toll. Do you know it?"

"I've heard the name."

"You were in our church," she said. "But you're not a Cephalist, are you?"

"A what?"

"Do you worship the Two-Headed Martyr?"

"No."

Mirth shrugged. "Every settlement has its own gods. The Two-Headed Martyr is ours. Do you have a god?"

"No."

"None? Rituals, religion—none?"

"Well, yes," said Corpse. "My tribe...," he tried to come up with the words to describe the culture that seeped into his bones from infancy. "My tribe has beliefs, but no gods."

Mirth nodded sagely. "None I've met from the Malwoods have been particularly religious."

"Our belief is that we are machines made against our will."

"Grim."

"Yes, I suppose so," said Corpse. "And what of your martyr?"

"The Two-Headed Martyr was killed because one of her heads spoke the past, and the other spoke the future. They would convene and create the present. She was staked by a cruel lord who refused to listen."

"Grim."

"Yes, but isn't it all?"

"What did your martyr see of the future?"

"Many things. Different iterations of our own lives, some tragic, some fantastical. When we die, we believe we pass from one realm to the next. To live a life that is the same, but different."

"For us, release from life is the greatest gift."

"Oh? Then why are any of you alive?"

"It's our own personal tragedy," explained Corpse. "It is not easy to take another life. It is not easy to take one's own life. Some do it, yes, and no doubt should they be lauded. But for many of us, it is not easy. Our mind's revolt at the idea."

"Indeed, my sorrowful friend, that is a tragedy." She smiled at him. "I do not know where your journey takes you, but I know that you could use a good night's sleep. Have a room tonight."

"Really, there's no need."

"No, there isn't. But I am a machine that is made for kindness. There is nothing I can do."

"I've yet to meet that sort of machine. I'm not an easy thing to be kind to. You may fail."

"Then let me fail. And I'll let you sleep."

3
IN DROSS TOLL

In the Malwoods, there were no inns. They went to bed in graves, near the bones of their progenitors. The Drunken Prophet's accommodations were more luxurious than anything Corpse had experienced.

Awaking in a bed stuffed with feathers, Corpse heated bathwater and bathed for the first time in weeks. The water was purifying, burning his skin till it shined pink as a newborn's. With the remaining bathwater—now rendered a murky gray, he plunged his clothes and scrubbed them furiously. Afterwards, he laid them out by the fireplace.

It was early and his clothes were damp when Mirth knocked on the door, then opened it without concern for his privacy. Corpse stood nude and watched the fire.

"You need clothes?" she asked.

"I have clothes."

"If you can call them that. Give me a moment."

Mirth left in a hurry, toddling down the hallway. Minutes later, she returned.

"Now, this won't get you into the Count's court—not

that anyone in their right mind would want to be—but it'll keep your pecker from freezing off."

Corpse examined the clothes. "Thank you," he said. It was a simple pair of trousers and shirt, but they were clean and soft to the touch.

Corpse lifted his clothes from the fireplace, and packed them into a satchel. But, as he was about to grab his sword, Mirth touched his shoulder. When he turned around, she was inches away from his face.

"Your clothes are not yet dry," she said. "Put them back."

Corpse's fingers lingered over the wet clothes in his satchel.

"Go on, let them dry," she said.

He unpacked them and placed them back beside the fire.

When Corpse turned back to her, her lips pressed into his. In shock, the stranger stumbled backwards.

She stepped out of her dress with the sort of grace that comes only from repetition. Corpse had never seen anyone so old. Her body was scarred, splitting at the seams. Her gray hair hung over her small breasts, her stomach betrayed lightning bolts of pink flesh, of electric history.

Gently, she approached again. Closing the distance, bringing his hands to hers. Corpse relented, tentatively holding her hips.

"What if you have a child?"

"I will not," she whispered in his ear. "I cannot have children anymore. I am too old for children."

"Too old?"

"Yes, that's what happens when we're too old." His hands trembled against her, but his cock was erect. She reached down to it, stroking it through his trousers. "Have you not been with a woman?"

"No, not a woman," said Corpse.

"Would I be your first?"

He nodded.

"Okay," she said.

Urges are such that they are not easily conquered. They build, they fester. To deny them is to give them strength. Corpse moaned softly in Mirth's ear, caressing her breasts, biting into her neck. Before long, she spread herself on the bed, guiding him into her. In those moments, his past haunted him, while his future promised that the haunting would never end. But in the present, she was beautiful, her skin was his blessing. Inside of her, he felt as if it was whispering to his own future, in defiance. Her past was sublimity; mighty and godly. More powerful even than her martyr; more powerful than his grave.

With a pang of terror, he released inside of her. He tensed, his whole body in rictus as Mirth wrapped her slender legs around him. When she cooed in his ear, "It's okay, it's okay," it was as if she could read his mind. His body went limp. Tenderly, he kissed her open mouth.

Mirth stood, pulling the dress over her shoulders, offering a coy half-smile while Corpse did the same.

"So, you'll be going now," she said.

"Yes."

"Okay."

"Thank you for your hospitality."

A laugh escaped the woman's voice. "My hospitality."

"No, no. Not like—" but Corpse too gave into rare laughter. "That wasn't what I meant."

"I know it, love. Are you alright?"

"I should be, shouldn't I?"

"It doesn't mean anything. Not if you don't want it—" Corpse placed his sword by his side. The leather strap squeaked as he tied it to his belt. It was a light thing, a swift killing tongue. The guard was a chaotic twist of metal, an explosion of bent angles and liquidity.

Corpse's face went solemn. "Have you seen a blade like this?"

Mirth nodded.

"I'm sorry. Truly." Corpse gathered the rest of his things quickly. He lingered by the doorway, his mouth opened slightly. Mirth had sat up and she was about to say something also—maybe something tender, kind; something wise and soothing; something that could burrow in the stranger's chest and nestle around his heart—when a loud crash sounded from downstairs.

"What's that?" she said.

Shouting, smashing, fighting. Their eyes locked. It took only a second for her to understand.

Corpse turned the doorknob, his head lowered. "My reputation has followed me," he said.

Mirth blinked away some small wetness in her eyes— the fruits of sympathy and curiosity. The eyes of someone who loved everything she looked at, and desired nothing more than for it to persist in perpetuity.

"Goodbye," he said. "And thank you."

But before she could respond, the man named Corpse had left.

4

WEAK SHACKLES

THERE WAS NO SENSE FIGHTING. Corpse too was afraid to die. They dragged him out into the street. He did not dare look back.

THE CASTLE that loomed over Dross Toll was a great onyx behemoth. On the outside, Graytoll was more like a gravestone than a home. It was tall and rectangular, ordained with ornate carvings of open-mouthed devils and twin-headed maidens battling in stasis. Its doors were tall and arched, made from dark wood that was so heavy, two strong men stood by to open and close them on command. The windows were mere slits, and out from these dark slashes shined the bright eyes of anxious archers. Inside, one grand room opened to another grander room. Fireplaces tall enough to house a towering man roared in each, animating the stone walls with their licking tongues.

Corpse was flanked by seven men, all strong and gruff and shaken by what they'd seen. They had stripped him of his weapons over the dead guard's transported body, while asking rushed questions. "Did you do this?" "Who did this?" "Are you a sorcerer?" "Where's the man who did this?"

Of course, he gave no answer. The man had done nothing wrong; he did not want to die.

A fist sailed into his stomach and he felt the air release from his body. The cats hissed and growled, ready to pounce if he were to run. The rest of the uneasy guardsmen took their turns with him in the street as others watched through curious eyes.

When he was soft and pliable, but still able to walk, they marched him through the streets, a collar tied to his neck as the cats set the pace. If the collar grew tight, he'd be pulled forward, dragged along through the muck. He learned quickly to maintain a jog, lest he wish to feel his skin burn from friction.

Inside the castle, the men seemed more at ease. As they led him deeper and deeper into Dross Toll's fortress, they laughed and joked more. "Keep that firelight in your eyes, boy," said one guard. "It'll be the last light you ever see."

Corpse's face remained a mask.

At the far corner of the dungeon, in what felt like a mile below the surface, Corpse met the hard stone floor of a cell with a sudden and vicious push.

Again, the guards laughed.

"A fitting room for a man named Corpse."

Corpse did not disagree, instead, he breathed deep, letting the cool, damp air fill his lungs.

"He's not a talker, is he?"

"No, I reckon he's not."

"That'll be good then. There's plenty to not talk about down here."

Their laughter echoed through the blackness of the dungeon. A hint of a torch danced far away. Corpse pressed his face against the iron bars.

As soon as he did, it vanished.

THE BLOOD SLAKED HIS THIRST. A delicate taste of the beyond. Blood on the taste buds. Blood on his face. Blood in his veins. He'd been screaming for hours. For each body he sent to the grave, his mouth opened in a wretched scream. He screamed for both him and the ones who died by his sword. The ones who had their lives' taken—for both their loss and their triumph. Corpse screamed for each of them because they met their final fate with suddenness and bravery. And he screamed for himself too—for the envy he felt, for the fear that mixed with his blood, for the realization that it was not him on the ground, but it could've been.

When killing, when freeing those that stood before him, his mind floated off into richer, moonlit pastures. It was the closest thing to calm he knew.

They dragged the bodies into the town square and then came the sorrow that accompanied the digging. Every man, woman, and child in the Malwoods dug their own grave at a young age. Often, they cried while doing it. And on the battlefield, they showed their slain the same respect. The work of a priest was not done until the dead were buried. So, Corpse joined the others. He stabbed his shovel into the earth. Tattooed killers with sinewy arms and blackened blades at their hips all weeping as they dug deep graves, each individual given its resting place.

And when the bodies were buried and nothing was left of them but the blood that washed over the battlefield, it was time to remove the stain of civilization.

The village was small. The farmers had slept in after a long day of work. The children dreamt. They did not know it was their day to die. But that was for the better. Corpse held a torch in his hand. The village was silent, just as it had been when they crept through the night. And but for one violent, death rattle, it was quiet again.

Corpse touched the flame to one hut, then another and another. As dawn came, black smoke kissed the horizon. They had been successful. There was no life here.

* * *

Corpse woke suddenly. There was light.

"You'll die here, you know?"

Corpse was tempted to respond. To say, *what difference does it make where I die?* but they were not speaking to him.

Another body was being hauled into the blackness, thrown into the cell beside his.

"Go on there, get to rotting," said the guard, already leaving—his orange, flickering face floating away. Leaving them in blackness.

The man whimpered. He said, "Hello? Is there anyone here."

Corpse bit his tongue, then said. "Yes, I'm here."

"Who are you?"

The voice was familiar, accented. Corpse recalled it immediately.

"A foreigner. Like you."

"I'm sorry," he said, finally.

"For what?"

"You were going to kill him, because of what he was going to do to me."

"I was."

"You would not be in here if it weren't for me."

Even though the bard could not see, Corpse shrugged. "It does not matter to me. I still plan to kill them."

"How? My magic has limits. I am not impervious."

Corpse leaned against the cold, wet rocks behind. "What is your name, bard?"

"Jessa," he said.

"I am Corpse."

"A strange name."

"I hear that often," he said "How did they find you?"

"I was foolish. I was caught."

"And you couldn't do to that man what you did to the guard?"

"No," said Jessa. "Sorcery has its cost."

"What is this cost?"

"For me, it is time. Hours, minutes, years off my natural life."

Corpse nodded.

"But you have not told me your plan, Corpse."

"I do not have a plan, not yet. Surely you do not wish to die here?"

"No," said Jessa. "I don't wish to die. Would it be easy to lift a key from a guard? Of course. It may only cost me minutes. But I still have to leave through the rest of the castle. I am not a fighter and while I could ask you to fight for me, I do not think even a warrior—of which I sense you are—would be able to fight an entire kingdom."

"You'd be surprised."

"Maybe so. But I would be foolish to place myself into a position where I might need to forfeit decades of my lifespan."

"Of course," said Corpse. "I understand."

"So, we are stuck, at least for a moment. In the blackness of a grave, bound by shackles that can be overcome easily, but will not be."

"It sounds like a tiring predicament. To be able to do whatever you wish, but having the discipline not to."

"In the Ghostcliffs, this is how we are. We know no other way. Where are you from, stranger?"

"The Malwoods."

Silence. Corpse waited for his new cellmate to speak.

His voice turned vicious. "I should turn you inside out," he said, "like that animal of a guard."

"I could not stop you."

"Zealots," he spat.

"Yes," said Corpse. "We are known as such."

"Merciless. We tell stories about you. We tell our children that Malwood marauders come in the night with skulls reflected in their pupils, that they take life wantonly, without care."

"There is much care in what we do," said Corpse.

"Is there? Cutting the throats of newborns is care?"

"For us, it is."

Jessa retreated to the opposite side of his cell. "If I'm escaping, it will be without you."

"I am not in the Malwoods now, you notice. I roam freely. I cannot help where I was born."

"None of us can," said Jessa. "But we can help what we do."

5
IN THE COUNCIL OF COUNT VINIRI

THE COUNT SAT on a throne elevated above his council. A long, wood table, lacquered to the point of being a mirror. When Count Viniri asked a question and no one answered, he'd use this time to admire his reflection. Black hair with strips of shining white, a sharp pointed goatee, arched eyebrows, and a heavy golden chain that ended in the Two-Headed Martyr around his neck.

Today, the question which prompted this awkward silence was, "Why are these men still alive?"

The first guard, the boldest of them, sat closest to his Count. "We know of your taste for torture. We were simply providing an opportunity."

The count raised an eyebrow. "These are dangerous men, yes? La'Dir?"

"Yes."

"And they are so dangerous that rather than dispose of them when you had a chance, you decided to bring them into my home?"

"We do not think they're a danger now. They are weak, feeble."

"Yes, so feeble that only today one of them turned a royal guard into soup. Thank you, La'Dir, your analysis is stunning."

La'Dir grit his teeth. "We can kill them now, if you prefer."

"No, no, no," said the Count, with a wave of his hand. "You've gone through the trouble. I might as well see them."

"They may be working in concert. They could be carrying out a plot."

Viniri remembered the tales he was told as a child, of his father and grandfather—dressed in shining silver, commanding forces against bandits from the Northern Shore. "You think so?" he asked, barely able to mask the hope on his tongue.

"Why else would we have two foreigners within the limits of Dross Toll?"

"That's a good point, La'Dir." He smiled with sharp yellow teeth. "I take everything back. You are wise beyond my opinion of you."

"Thank you, sir."

"I will meet them in the great hall," said Count Viniri. "And I will do what I please with them there."

When La'Dir left, Count Viniri took one last look at himself in the shiny wood of his table. As he eyed the lines in his face, he broke his gaze with the reflection. Alone, he stood, examining the blade taken from the foreigner. It was strange, heavy, but well-used. The Count weighed it in his own hand and slashed at a phantom enemy. It sliced through the air with ease. It was a good weapon, it had likely seen much blood.

Joy rippled across his countenance. "I will have this invader's head."

6

THE SEEDS OF CHAOS

"Well now, have you made fast friends?" laughed the guard. "Two skeletons, to be unearthed in a millennia. A future defined by the past."

Corpse saw Jessa huddled in the corner of his cell, a hateful expression smeared across his lips.

"We're taking you to see the Count. Do be on your best behavior."

The door opened and Corpse thought of barreling forward, wrestling a sword away from one of the armored guards, and gutting them like a beast. But as he imagined that outcome, he also saw the more likely one—that he would be killed, and quick.

So, he let them surround him. Jessa kept his eyes focused ahead of him, clearly not wanting to meet Corpse's gaze.

They led them through dank corridors and extravagant rooms, gilded from floor to ceiling, through a private monastery decorated with detailed paintings of the Two-Headed Martyr, weaving a tapestry that Corpse was sure was meant to be the present, while its heads turned opposite of each other, communing with the past and future.

From there, they passed through more stone mazes, before arriving in a great hall where each of their footsteps echoed.

On the opposite end of the hall was a man dressed in a red fur cloak that trailed on the ground. It wrapped around his neck with a gold clasp, two heads each biting a length of cloth.

Corpse eyes narrowed. The Count held his sword.

"Kneel," said one of the guards. Someone kicked him, he fell forward. Jessa followed, appearing more indignant by the second.

The Count swished Corpse's sword through the air. He did not look at them at first, nor did he seem particularly eager to sate any burgeoning curiosity. The Count reminded Corpse of a bored housecat. "You have come to Dross Toll and made a sort of racket here," he said, finally. "The only reason, I can assume, you have come here is to cut off my head and claim Dross Toll for whatever pathetic tribe you hail from. So, please, do tell me who sent you."

Jessa said, "I have not been sent for you. I was wrongly attacked by one of your guards."

"And why was that?"

"I don't know, I was playing music."

"Poorly, I take it."

"He attacked me and I defended myself," said Jessa. "If you allow me to leave, you will never see me again."

The Count yawned. "And you, stranger, what brings you here?"

"I was only passing through."

The Count laughed. "So we have two people here, both involved in the brutal killing of a royal guard, and they just happen to be passing through. How coincidental. No, no, I don't believe it."

"I believe you do believe it," said Corpse.

"Oh?"

"Yes, I don't believe you care if we're here to kill you or not. I don't believe you see us as threats. I don't believe you see anything as a threat."

"And why is that?"

"Your city is well guarded. Your archers are paranoid and eager. You look like a man who has taken great care to keep himself protected. But there is little here to protect. Dross Toll has no ports, what riches it has is dwarfed by other cities. The people here are here because they were born here, no other reason. New settlers, with visions of other lives, would not stay here and you would not want them to stay. For they would sow the dischord that would put your leisurely, paranoid life into chaos. Be truthful, Count, that is why we are here. Because we represent to you this seed of chaos."

Count Viniri licked his lips. "You are the man called Corpse," he said. "The death-obsessed savage. Your people sleep in graves and you have the *nerve* to question how Dross Toll lives. Of course." He laughed. "You will not complete your foul mission."

A guard grabbed him. Corpse struggled, his muscles bulging as he threw himself free from the first man, but not the next, or the next after that. Their arms wrapped around him, he kicked his feet out into the air like a petulant toddler. Jessa too was held, although his body made no argument.

"If you wish to free us, now is your time," he said to the Bard.

Viniri approached, blade drawn and hungry. It brushed against Corpse's chest, slicing easily through his shirt.

"Now! Sorcerer! Do something!" Corpse bellowed. The guardsmen held him back.

Jessa closed his eyes, but did nothing.

Viniri twisted the point in his chest. The wounds were only skin deep, for now. But each time the tip met his flesh, Viniri pushed it slightly deeper. Blood ran in thick red rivulets down Corpse's chest.

"I do not want to die," he muttered.

"He can not help you," said Viniri.

He craned his neck to the bard. "Jessa," said Corpse. "A small favor perhaps." The guards kept his arms straight beside him, but as he spoke, he straightened. "Surely, my sword would only cost a minute or two?"

Jessa seemed to weigh this possibility. "Yes," he said, finally.

The sword twisted out of Viniri's hand and into Corpse's, floating weightless between the two as if it'd been forged from air alone. He swung widely, dashing forward, throwing the guards off him. Corpse wondered as he dove if this was some small help from Jessa, a minute or two more to load the dice in his favor. Viniri turned on helpless feet to see Corpse at the end of the hall, standing with the Count's throne at his back. Three guards drew their swords while the other three held Jessa in a vice grip.

Viniri retreated, making distance between himself and the man from the Malwoods.

"I do not wish to end your lives today," said Corpse. "Release my friend from the Ghostcliffs and let us leave, peacefully."

The Count shook his head. He turned to the guards holding Jessa. "Kill the sorcerer."

A blade slid across Jessa's throat. The guards released him to the ground, where he fell heavily, holding his neck and jerking across the floor in violent spasms. Blood seeped out in a red pool.

With three extra blades at their disposal, the guards became more bold in their advancement. Behind them, Count Viniri sneered with vicarious bloodlust.

"So be it," said Corpse. "Greet the worms."

He was fast. Faster than they could have imagined. He lunged first toward the right most enemy, low to the ground, somersaulting past his slicing blade. By the time he sprung up, his own sword was already in mid swing. The guard's eyes widened and the five others twisted to see the blade cutting cleanly through their comrade's throat.

A geyser erupted from his neck, painting Corpse's face with the color of rage.

As the first body hit the floor, Corpse parried a broad strike. The guards were used to carrying swords, but not using them. It only took one parry to push the blade off to the side, leaving the guards wrists exposed to Corpse's fearsome blade.

The chime of metal hitting the floor rang through the hall, accompanied by the dull thud of a severed hand.

The guard screamed.

Corpse watched him hide behind his fellow warriors, staring in shock at his bloodied stump, his mouth agape and cheeks pale.

The next guard was a better swordsman, but predictable. He parried each of Corpse's initial strikes, but failed to probe for any weakness. The guard was joined by two more. Viniri edged closer to the exit. "Kill him!" he cried. "Kill this corpsefucker!"

One guard cocked his head to hear what his Count had said. The next moment his entrails were at his feet.

Corpse made distance between the two, his blade out in front of him, a cold dare to the Count's guards. One they were compelled to take.

Corpse said, his voice a soft whisper, "I am giving you a choice, here and now. Retreat or join your brethren."

Nervously, one of them searched from the corner of their eye for their friend's head. As they weighed their decision, the other guard waved his bloody stump as phlegmy screams erupted from his throat.

Viniri answered for them. "If you do not kill him, I will have you killed." His voice was even and cold.

The guards knew he spoke the truth.

One of them dived toward Corpse, a clumsy recreation of what they'd witnessed earlier. The man's outstretched blade was supposed to cut him at the knee, but Corpse stepped back, letting the sword swish past him, while he thrust his through the man's throat.

Corpse pulled the blade.

Blood, blood, more blood. More blood than he'd seen in weeks.

A welcome return, he thought.

The last two stood quivering, their blades shaking in the air like candlelight.

One powerful beat and the first guard's sword fell to the floor. He ended him easily, pushing the tip of his blade through his sternum into his heart. Corpse listened closely, to the grating sound of metal on bone. The man fell.

The final guard took one step back, then another and another. He was a weakling. He had spoken of death, but never seen it. The Count slipped out of the Great Hall, no doubt running frantically to a new wing to gather more expendable talent.

The guard turned, his legs spread as if to run—

But the blood.

He slipped, falling forward, his sword outstretched.

CRUNCH!

He moaned, flipping over, holding his nose. Corpse thought it might be broken. He couldn't tell now if the guard was covered in his own blood or that of his comrades.

Corpse followed the man as he edged backwards on his hands until his back met the door.

"Close your eyes," said Corpse. "If you wish."

Tears fell, he held out a hand as if to say: *no!*

The last thing the guard would see was a flash of brilliant silver. And then, briefly, red.

7

A CLEVER RUSE

"HE'S IN HERE!" Viniri called from the other side of the door.

The sound of hundreds of guards and their footsteps echoed through the hall. Corpse had shoved the shaft of a brazier through the handles to give him time, but it would only be a matter of minutes before the men charged—turning the great, ornate door into great, ornate splinters.

"Gather up! He's trapped!"

Corpse searched the room. There were two great stained glass windows, each twice as tall as he. They depicted a glowering figurehead looming over the freshly staked form of the Two-Headed Martyr.

Corpse touched the cold glass, palms flat. It was about fifty feet off the ground, high enough to shatter at least a bone or two. Down the slick gray walls of the castle was an embankment that became a small valley, everything beyond that was green pines and firs.

Outside:

CRRSH! CRRSH! CRRSH!

The guards had found a battering ram, no doubt.

He swung his sword at the image of the king and his slain prophet, shattering it into glittering dust.

CRRSH! CRRSH! CRRSH!

One foot on the edge, then the other. Corpse stood on unsteady feet, looking down toward the earth, wondering if it would make for a fitting grave.

He closed his eyes and remembered warm sunsets and fleeting moments of laughter, of explosive mania, of melancholy. He remembered Mirth's body underneath his.

CRRSH! CRRSH! CRRSH!

The door buckled. The men's voices rang louder.

"We could make it," said a voice.

Corpse spun around. A smile crept over his lips. "How much time did it cost you to fake that wound?"

Jessa stood weakly, his eyes darting to the door and back.

"Enough. But not too much. Killing a man takes the most time of all. I did not have to kill anyone, I only needed to stop the blade before it went too deep. Enough to bleed and no more." He stopped, rubbing at the wound. "I owe you a favor, it seems. So, here it is, death worshiper. We will jump, and we will not die. That is what I can offer you."

Corpse nodded slowly. "Thank you, Jessa," he said. "Truly."

The door cracked again, the bolts on its hinges pulling from the wall in clouds of dust and cobwebs.

Jessa approached the window. "Jump with me, death worshiper."

Without warning, Jessa leapt, and Corpse followed.

His stomach plunged into his throat. He was not accustomed to heights, despite living amongst the trees. But as he fell, he slowed slightly. It was as if he jumped into dry water.

Corpse marveled at the stranger's magic, feeling its warmth course around him. Magic was rare in the Malwoods—rarely used outside of the seers who brought messages from abroad.

His feet touched down lightly.

A great crash sounded, followed by the boom of the Great Hall's door falling. It echoed like thunder. Jessa had already run for the trees, sliding down the slope of the valley into the wilderness. Corpse craned his neck to see soldiers gathered at the broken window.

One drew an arrow across his bow, notching it and pulling back.

Corpse ran into the woods, and as he did, he heard the arrow's whistle, and many more, docking into the trees.

* * *

BEHIND HIM, the sounds of riding cats echoed abound. Jessa had gone. Corpse figured the sorcerer had learned ways of hiding himself, or knew that the strange man from the Malwoods would be an easier target to distract the guards. They would follow Corpse and forget the man from the Ghostcliffs. They might not even notice his body missing from the carnage in the Great Hall, or worse, they might assume that Corpse stole it as some part of a strange death ritual.

It was a good plan, a clever ruse, if true.

But the woods were Corpse's home. He had been trained to live outside of civilization—to be a traveler on the road of carnage.

He ran on light feet through a stream, up the other side of the valley; at a high vantage point he turned to see the men following him. They were miles away now. The cats were sniffing for him, drinking in his blood before they could taste it. He heard them hiss at each other, communing in that vicious feline manner. They would lose him at the stream. Hopefully then, the soldiers would give up, go back to their master, and assume his death.

On the other side of the valley, Dross Toll rolled out in a sea of small houses, dwarfed by its church and castle. Corpse was glad to leave them both.

8

UNENDING STRIFE

They slept under the stars. *It was not their custom to erect tents or take cover. If they were to die in the night: good.*

Corpse did not sleep soundly though. They had not been thorough. He could smell the cooking flesh. It wafted into his nostrils and stung the back of his throat. He closed his eyes tight.

Perhaps it was a child who had been hiding under their bed during the attack, blinking wet eyes before the smoke made them pass out, before the fat beneath their flesh crackled and popped. It was a poor way to die.

Sleep did not come. Instead, he counted the stars until they disappeared.

He was solving a puzzle. Slowly, through the prior weeks, he had begun excavating himself. Ideas in their infancy pushed out from their eggs and yawned inside of him. Privately, when he could, he nurtured these thoughts. Partly, because he had never nurtured anything at all. And also, because he felt like he was on the verge of something. Two pieces, so close to fitting together. He only had to work at it a little longer.

But the morning came before any resolution and their

general called their orders. "Up!" she said. "Get up! There are more to liberate."

Corpse and the other priests stood, shaking off the sleep with the earth. There were no more than thirty of them, many miles from home.

General Loss stood before them. Her eyes were a dead gray, her hair had been shaved down to a prickle. On the side of her skull, a coffin was tattooed in smudgy black ink. Her right hand laid on the pommel of her sheathed sword. "There is another settlement within these woods," she said. She pointed across the prairie to a wall of black trees. "Our scouts spotted footprints. They have likely heard word of last night's extermination, they may try to deny themselves their release."

"How many more villages before we go home?" he asked.

"We will continue our liberation until we ourselves die," she said with kindness. "If there are none in the woods, we will leave the woods and go to the desert, or the rocky shores, or some other hellish bastion for life." Her words were not venomous, but measured, considered, inevitable.

"The last battalion of clergy returned to the Malwoods," he said.

"Each battalion is at the behest of its leader," said Loss. "And as your leader, I have decided that we will not return. We will keep fighting for our and others' freedom." She took a step toward Corpse, and placed a hand on his shoulder. "Worry not, brother. This pain will not last."

Corpse bowed his head, concealing a deep discomfort. "I am grateful, General."

The other warriors looked to each other quietly, accepting their fate. Some had likely expected this. They had elected Loss as their general precisely because of the strength of her will. They had volunteered to proselytize and if their mission begat death, then so be it.

General Loss stared into the trees. "These people are just like us," she whispered. "They were born to fear, born to starve, born to hurt, born to die. What a sad state." She sighed and marched forward. Her priests followed.

* * *

Corpse awoke to the sound of crackling pine needles.

Voices.

"I'm sure he's dead," said a man.

Corpse stared at the wet moss in the hollowed log he'd found as shelter.

"If he's not?"

"He will not be coming back here anytime soon."

"You think so? Have you not heard the tales of vengeance in the Malwoods?"

A pause. "No."

The other man sighed. "They had a warrior once, named Meatlace, who left his village to bring death upon any who he met. He was a wanderer, much like this man here. He wandered the trails and roads to find men and women that he could gut in the wilds. He'd bury them, yes. He'd sing a mournful tune, of course. Children, their mothers, blacksmiths—they rot underground because of Meatlace's lust for death. But, there was one warrior, a knight, an honorable man, who crossed his path. Of course, Meatlace was from the Malwoods, so he had no such knowledge of honor. There are no knights in that pessimistic tribe. They are a bleak bunch—they know only of despair. Meatlace surely saw this man dressed in silver and thought him nothing more than a pathetic pretender."

"A pretender? A knight?"

"Yes, that's right. Those of the Malwoods do not use

armor, they see it as comical. In their vision, death is abso-lute. Why deny its power?"

Corpse heard the other man shudder. "And?"

"Well, they did battle of course. The knight and Meat-lace fought and it was a vicious fight, surely. Those strange people from the forest, for all their degeneracy, are indeed warriors of the highest caliber. They fear so much that they fear nothing, they say. The two traded blow after blow but it was the knight that ended up disarming the man named Meatlace. Because the knight honored a code, he would not kill an unarmed man. He left the tattooed ruffian alone in the woods, sure that would be the end of it."

"But it wasn't, I assume."

The footsteps grew closer. Corpse was sure one of the men stood right beside his log, perhaps even resting on it.

"You assume correctly. Meatlace was an exceptional tracker, a predator trained to conquer what he most feared and most desired—a release from his own mental anguish. So, he followed the knight home to his kingdom—listening, investigating; hearing him speak to his family and friends. He grew his hair out and found work in the kitchen of the castle. He was baking bread and stirring stews!" The man laughed, short and sharp. "Yes, the bastard was smart. The knight had forgotten him, or nearly so. And he didn't remember until he found the bodies of his wife and daughter dismembered in his quarters. Angry, he rushed to the king to mount an investigation. Only, when he pushed the doors open, the king was no more. His head rolled to his armored feet and on his throne sat the vagabond known as Meatlace. He fell to his knees, weeping, he removed his helmet and the stranger from the Malwoods raised his blade, and you know what he said?"

The other man had hardly exhaled. "No, what?"

"He said, 'You are most welcome.'"

Corpse laid still. He held his breath. It was an old story, one told by firelight.

"Fuck the Martyr," said one of the guards.

"Aye. But we'll find him. Viniri's got a taste for blood, he does. He'll have our heads if we don't find the prick."

"It never ends, this life of woe."

"Fuck off," said the other guard. "Let's check the valley again, maybe we missed his tracks."

Corpse listened closely to their footsteps. He did not move for another hour.

* * *

As night fell, he traveled by the silver light of a hungry moon. Corpse was determined to put as many miles between him and Dross Toll as possible.

He hiked through the night, until the sun rose on a gilded horizon. The forest was a strange place, he realized. A stranger place than even he knew.

Trees scraped the painting where some kept their gods. Great jackals with unhinged jaws snapped fish in half, leaving a gleaming waterfall of pink roe in their wake. And in front of him, was a tower—alone in the woods.

It was not made of brick or stone or wood. The structure moved—in and out, in and out—as if it were breathing. In the early pink of the sunrise, he couldn't tell if the thing's color was that of the light, or if it were truly the color of flesh.

9

A BODY

THE GREAT HALL had been swept out, a large canvas sheet was nailed to the wall to cover the broken window. Count Viniri sat on his throne for only a minute before insisting the meeting be moved somewhere else.

"It's drafty here, cold. We can have the meeting in my own quarters."

La'Dir nodded. "Of course, sire."

Viniri seemed incapable of staring at the flapping wall of canvas, just as he seemed incapable of appearing at his guard's funerals. "They're dead," he said. "That's all there is to it. They're living other lives now. Praise to the Martyr." And as he said it, he stormed out of the room and demanded a full extra hour of practice with his fencing instructor. Afterwards, he declared to La'Dir that no one in the castle would rest until the man named Corpse was brought to justice.

La'Dir, well acquainted with his master's erratic temperament, agreed.

"You are a commander, I ask only that you command," said Count Viniri, soaking from his steaming tub.

"I cannot make men find what they have not found."

Viniri's pupils became pinpricks.

"We will keep looking," said La'Dir.

"Have you questioned villagers?"

"Yes, I have. Personally."

Viniri motioned for La'Dir to continue. "Please, don't keep me waiting."

"He came into town and stayed at an inn."

"Which inn?"

"The Drunken Prophet."

"The only place that'd take him, no doubt."

"The owner—"

"Mirth," he spat.

"Yes, Mirth. She invited him to stay on hospitality. She fed him, clothed him, took him to a church service, and made love to him before he left."

Viniri's nose crinkled. "She's old enough to be his grandmother."

"Aye," said La'Dir. "I shudder to think of what love looks like between those two."

"Have you tortured her yet?"

La'Dir tried his best to obscure his astonishment. "Torture?"

"She's the only person who was close to him."

"Her father."

"Her father is dead."

"His wealth is not."

"She's been a thorn in my side since I've taken the crown," he said restlessly.

"She commands power and respect. I would be careful to make an enemy of her."

"She's already my enemy." Viniri splashed water toward La'Dir, who stood motionless. "But I see your point."

"She is worried," he said. "She told me as much. The people like her, they drink her ale and eat her food, but they can only handle so much eccentricity. The villagers saw what happened to that guard. Many of them can't sleep anymore. Nightmares are running rampant. Rumors have spread from the castle, they know that he has killed."

"And what do they say of me?"

La'Dir bit his tongue. "Nothing. They say nothing. They speak only of the strange man and his penchant for murder."

"You're a liar, Captain. But I do love your lies."

"Tomorrow morning, we'll send fifty of our best and we will find your Corpse," said La'Dir. "And after, we will parade his head down the streets." They had known each other for too long, La'Dir thought. Their conversations were more or less predestined. He knew what the Count wanted from him.

"To rapturous applause," said Viniri.

"Yes," said La'Dir. "To rapturous applause."

* * *

Mirth peered from behind the curtains, into the streets. "They're still here," she said. "You reckon they're ever gonna leave?"

Garrt wiped water out of a glass. "Not likely. Praise to the Martyr, Mirth. You've really done it now."

She cast him a harsh look and backed away from the window. Since she'd been questioned, she felt like she was being watched continuously. For the last day and night, the Drunken Prophet had been filled with guards. Sure, they'd paid for their drinks, but she could tell they were *listening*. Outside, in the street, they were never far away. They held their spears as if they were to be ready to slay her at a moment's notice.

She sighed. "I haven't a clue what I've done. What do they think I know at this point?"

"Did he say where he was going?"

"No," she said. "He wasn't much of a talker."

"I can even see that," said Garrt. "Polite fellow though, didn't strike me as a killer, despite his..." he circled his own head with his index finger. "Tattoos."

"If he did what they said he did, they had it coming. The boy was on a mission of some sorts."

"He told you that?"

"No, I drew my own conclusions. He's looking for something."

"Treasure? Could that be why the Count—"

"No," she said sharply. "Something else."

"He's a priest then?"

"That's what he would call himself, I believe."

Garrt poured them both a glass of frothy ale. "You're thinking of something dire, aren't you?"

Mirth took a sip of beer and smiled, despite herself. "You can read me like a book."

"Well, out with it. Let's hear this grand plan. You going out into the woods to find Corpse? To warn him? He's long gone by now, most likely."

"No, no. Nothing like that. I'm old, Garrt. I wouldn't survive a night. I'm not going to do anything rash. I'm just going to send a letter."

Garrt cocked his head. "To whom?"

"An old friend," she said. "Fetch me a seer."

10

HEADLESS AND HAPPY

PLACATE STOOD sharp as Captain La'Dir's cat paced back and forth at the treeline. She held her hands like they said she should—straight beside her with pointed fingers—and looked out ahead. She listened to the captain—a doughy man who had become cruel through circumstance rather than birth—and tried to conjure the same rage he so effortlessly performed for them.

He said, "We will gut him like deer! We will feast from his bloody fucking innards! We will find the death worshiper and make sure he dies in helpless agony!"

"Yes, sir!" she yelled with the others.

As a girl, she had made the decision early on that she would like to be one of the Count's guards. Her parents encouraged her in her swordship, her riding. At sixteen, they took her on a trip into the woods where she made her first kill, outside the city of Dross Toll. Placate trembled when she cut the old vagrant's throat with the dagger, much as she trembled now, one year later, her first day wearing the Count's seal.

A man beside her said, "You're supposed to march now."

"Shit."

He was already a step ahead, she took extra long leaps to catch up. She held her spear tight, admiring how it glinted.

Captain La'Dir called from up ahead. "Leave no stone unturned! Check everything! He dies or we die."

Placate nodded very seriously. Her heart beat with the wings of a hummingbird. When she closed her eyes, she tried to imagine the man they were searching for as La'Dir described him. *Tall, fit. Close shorn hair, with visible skin ink —images of death and the grave. A dark beard. Deep, set eyes. Bronze skin. He carries a sword with a strange twisted guard.*

A young man said, "So, you think we'll find him?"

She called up ahead (because she was now part of this group, she was now one of the Count's guards), "We'll find him all right! We'll have his fucking head!"

* * *

THEY AREN'T A QUIET BUNCH, he thought.

Belly to the ground, he peered through ferns to the guards marching up the hill. They were maybe a half-mile out, but there were many of them. They hooted and hollered with undisciplined exuberance. Corpse would've been killed on the spot if he behaved this way in the Malwoods. No, these were no true warriors. They made up for skill with numbers.

A flash of red entered his brain. Words he didn't recognize slipped into his memory. He shook his head.

It was that *thing*. He rolled onto his back to look behind him. A tower, made of flesh. He could see its pores when he stood close. Faint, translucent hairs covered it like peach fuzz. It buzzed faintly, like an eldritch insect from a faraway land. But what was worse was the *thoughts* it planted inside of him.

Corpse scratched at his head.

I might be going mad, he thought.

The guards continued to scream their cries of desecration.

The tower breathed.

Mutilated horizons, screaming mouths, an infant bludgeoned against a rock. Blood in the river, soaking deep, tinting the pristine with its crimson. The sound of voices, people speaking. They said words he could not recognize in a tongue he did not know. And suddenly, time began to move along, to spread itself wide and thin in a black plane and his life began to take shape, to move at a glacial space. Eons between his first steps and first words. Millennia between his blinking eyes. Mountains eroded into sandy banks. The sky turned the color of blood. Civilizations came and went in the orgasmic gasp that created them. And then, the world became less and less and less. It became nothing.

Corpse shuddered.

The tower breathed.

A fog hung over his mind. He stumbled toward the voices and their bloodlust, if only to leave behind this strange and terrible artifact.

* * *

IT WAS midday before someone in front spotted bootprints. "Captain, over here!"

Placate rushed up front. Eager to impress, she followed the prints to a stream, hopped over it, and continued on the other side. Behind her, La'Dir dismounted his cat. She was glad he was here to watch her.

She stopped.

Another print at the foot of a tree.

Mud tracked up the side of the bark.

Placate craned her neck. Nothing. Only the swaying of needles.

"Over here," she called. "The bastard's up in the canopy!" Her voice rang loud and sharp. Placate, despite her name, had always been a brash child.

La'Dir's cat came bounding over first, its big nostrils flexing, its round yellow eyes staring upward. La'Dir and his soldiers followed.

Placate stood aside as the captain examined the tree for himself.

La'Dir whispered to his cat, then pointed up the tree. "Go," he said. "Drag him down."

The cat took an elegant step back, then leapt up the trunk, scaling it in seconds.

La'Dir slapped her on the shoulder. "Good work," he said. "I'll see you're rewarded."

Placate kept a grim countenance, nodding seriously, as her heart pounded. She fought hard to keep her grin buried deep.

They watched the foliage above. It had grown still shortly after the cat disappeared within it.

The forest went silent.

Each of the guards' breathing ceased.

Movement, a twitching of needles.

But then, no. Only a faint breeze.

"Trenk," he called. "Come down!"

More silence.

Placate took a step back, trying to find a new angle that could penetrate the thick canopy.

Then: the cat screamed.

They gathered their weapons and pointed at the tree—just as the needles exploded and a heavy body fell like an anvil.

Placate jumped back, startled. The cat fell in front of La'Dir's feet, its head twisted to stare at its own spine.

The squadron stood in mystified silence.

"Grab an ax," said La'Dir. "Start chopping. He's trapped!" He reached down to stroke his tawny cat.

Placate looked away, suddenly uncomfortable.

Within less than a half hour, the men had weakened the trunk. Up above, there was no sign of movement.

"Bring us our Corpse!" shouted La'Dir.

The tree swayed and a man with an ax kept his arm coiled like a spring, waiting for his captain's word.

"This is your last chance to come down!" La'Dir shouted.

Still nothing.

"Fine," he said. "Fell the tree—be ready when he comes!"

It took three more hard chops and the tree began to sway. With a gentle hand, the axeman pushed the trunk forward.

Placate gasped in amazement. The tree was so much larger than she imagined. So much taller than the canopy suggested.

With a resounding crash, La'Dir and his soldiers watched, surrounding the great heaping pile of needles and sap.

Placate held her spear tight. Waiting. Bloodlust rimmed her mouth. She was hungry. *I will be fed,* she told herself.

The pine needles burst in a dazzling display of firelight.

Hazy, blue smoke stung at her eyes. The tree was aflame.

She covered her face, frantically wiping away tears that ran down her cheeks.

"He's over there," said one of them. "He's running!"

La'Dir cursed. At the very end of the fallen pine, she could see the man running toward the horizon on feet so light they must have been air.

"STRING HIM BY HIS GUTS!" yelled Placate, and she ran too.

THEY WERE RUNNING AT HIM. Weren't they?

He watched them from afar, scratching his head, only a faint vision of the Red squirming in his brain. It got easier to think the further he got from the tower. *What foul magic lies in these woods?*

The visions were no more than pangs now. The screams had become whispers. The vistas had been swept away and they were like a dream—quickly forgotten upon waking. Time had, more or less, returned to normality. Corpse's usual sense of dread deepened, his limbs weak and his mind elastic.

The troops bounded up the hill, barreling toward him with spears pulled and the taste for blood on their tongues.

This image returned more of his senses. Corpse had long been trained in the art of war. He had killed as many men as time itself. But this did not seem right. Something was wrong.

A man ran past him.

"Jessa?" he said.

He turned to see the bard sprinting, darting between the trees. Corpse wondered if he had sacrificed yet more of his time on earth.

"Run!" yelled Jessa.

The soldiers were gaining, and now they *did* see Corpse.

"There he is, there's the bastard! Kill the Martyrfucker!"

Corpse yelled after Jessa, almost as an afterthought, "Don't go that way!" Then, he turned to face the soldiers, who were now less than the length of a felled tree from him.

He drew his sword, and then dipped down below into the underbrush, beneath a log, and then into a thin ditch, disguising himself in the tall grass. He crawled on his belly as the men rushed past him. One lingered, an older, gray-haired warhorse with a bent spear who looked as if he knew this forest was his grave.

The man stopped, he fell forward, hands on his knees, gasping for breath. The grass went up to his chest and Corpse kept low so that he could remain invisible. The guard looked up the hill toward the others, who were now far away, screaming and yelling for Corpse's blood. He rose behind the lone guard and sawed his blade through his windpipe. No sound came from the man. What once was life, became only heft as the old guard fell to the grass.

Corpse continued up the hill.

The bard had provided an opportunity. In the Malwoods, they called it the noose. Where the war would be fought on two or more sides, flanking the enemy, closing the circle tighter until they could not breathe—only die. Corpse silently ran up a log to where another guard trailed behind.

He leapt from the end of the log's roots, bringing his

sword down through the skull, burying it all the way into the guard's stomach.

When the body fell in the ferns, he went with it, sliding his blade from its bloody sheath.

A flame erupted up ahead. He heard a man wail, surely drinking fire that seared his lungs as he did. On the horizon, between the trees, Jessa's victim flailed wildly as skin began to pop and crisp. Corpse sniffed, letting the smell of roast pig whet his appetite for more blood.

At the top of the hill, Corpse watched them as they made their way through the tall grass of the valley. He could barely see the men, only their paths. Ahead of them, he saw Jessa, a lone shooting star, on the verge of vanishing.

The bard is a better tactician than I thought.

The trail of bent plants ended suddenly, where Jessa had likely dived low, leaving the trail cold. Corpse looked up from the valley, to the space beyond it, where the trees started again.

Above the treeline, there was only a hint of the tower. A fleshy steeple, shiny like scar tissue.

He retreated. One step at a time, lest he feel the sharp stab of the tower's memories.

Memories. He shuddered. *Was the tower alive?*

The guards, unwittingly, sliced their way through the tall grass, and Corpse stood still and silent as they hiked toward certain doom.

11

TRUE HORROR

"Can we stop for a minute?" asked one of the men.

La'Dir rubbed his head. "For a minute, no more."

They had exited the tall grass, spilling out from its denseness into the forest once again. Thick and inscrutable, a veritable wall of pine and lush needles. Placate's eyes twitched. She felt suddenly as if a worm was now chewing at her brain.

Still, she was eager. "I'll go up ahead," she said. "If I find him, I'll kill him."

The others laughed to themselves. They had been young and eager once too. They had once dreamed of being heroes, before the dull drudgery of reality rode them into tired boredom.

"If you find either of them, send them to hell, child," said one.

Placate smirked brazenly, then left the others to their rest.

The woods were dark.

But, they also seemed to glow.

* * *

IN A SMALL CAVE, in the light of a small fire, Corpse made peace with the twilight. He warmed his hands as the air cooled, eating roots he had washed in a stream. He thought, briefly, of Mirth, feeling a stirring in his loins that was as laced with melancholy as lust.

He remembered her skin, most of all. It was comfortable flesh, flesh that had lived. Corpse stared into the fire, somber realizations dancing between his ears.

He thought of driving his blade through his own stomach, ending his life right there in the cave, but he had thought this many times and never done it. He wondered if there would be a day when he would.

A twig snapped.

Corpse jumped to his feet, sword in hand.

He waited.

From the outer edge of the cave's opening, he saw a familiar face.

"Jessa," he said. "You've come to visit me."

"I smelled your smoke." The bard swallowed. "May I join you?"

"Please," said Corpse.

Jessa sat by the fire, the firelight warming his palms. "Did you kill any of the guards?" he asked.

"Only two. You?"

"One," he said. "But it cost me. Months, at least. Some fires only cost minutes, but humans don't burn from any fire. A special fire is needed."

"Sorry to hear that."

He shrugged. "Sometimes a demonstration of great power is necessary. Other times, it is wasteful."

"I have a feeling our friends will not last long either way," said Corpse.

"They're inexperienced."

"And the forest holds terror beyond their imagination."

Jessa paused. "What do you mean?"

"A structure, I think. Perhaps a beast. Maybe a life. Maybe nothing at all." said Corpse.

"Where was it?"

"A quarter mile or more further than where you lost them."

"Can you take me to it?"

"Are you seeking it?"

Jessa nodded. "It is why I have come here. To destroy it."

"I imagine our friends will find it soon."

"Tell me, death worshiper, did anything strange happen when you came to it?"

"Visions. Waking nightmares."

"Did you touch it? Did it open for you?"

"No, I left it quickly."

"You are wise then."

"What is it?" asked Corpse, unnerved by the gravity with which Jessa spoke.

The bard lost himself in the flames. "Do you know the people of the Ghostcliffs well?"

"Only what you have told me."

"We are sorcerers," said Jessa. "We make our home in the rock wall of a great cliff, a mile tall, that ends in the white raging waters of the Cammon Sea. If you were to visit our settlement by boat, you'd see our cliffs are chiseled with caves. Each of us has a home and each of our homes are connected by tunnels to the other. We are a close people, and we take in all sorts. In the Malwoods, I believe you have a similar custom. That your tribe is not bound by blood but belief, correct?"

Corpse grunted his affirmation.

"In the Ghostcliffs, we care only for knowledge. And that is what we seek and that is what we share amongst each other. That is why we live so closely, in our caves overlooking the sea. Years ago, arcane knowledge swept across the land and my people quickly mastered it. There is no Ghostcliffian who is not also a sorcerer—although it is a frequent matter of debate whether we rely too heavily on it. It's true, at least, that there are less of us than there used to be. Magic is its own vice, but I digress.

"A year ago, we had a strange man join our midst. We found him standing at the top of the cliff, breathing in the air of clouds. We thought that he meant to kill himself, and maybe he did. He did not tell us either way. His toes were off the edge of the cliff, kicking rocks down into the sea. One of our own found him and pulled him to safety. Quickly, it became apparent that this man was not in his right mind. He complained of strange dreams, he said that he did not come here on his own accord, but that he was *summoned* to us. Of course, none of us knew this man or had any idea where he came from. Not at first. He was a normal looking fellow, not obviously a warrior or a scholar. His hands were thick with calluses, his feet were dirty. We deduced that he might be a farmer of some sort. With some questions, we pinpointed his location here. In Dross Toll.

"When we asked for a name, he denied having one. When we asked for a home, he said he had no home. But that's not true, is it? Every man has a home, does he not?"

Corpse stared deep into Jessa's eyes, refusing to answer.

"He told us that he was on a quest, that he needed our help. That there was some infernal presence in the woods beyond his city, that it was threatening to change...*every-thing*. He claimed that it was merging the Martyr's realities —of course that is how we deduced he was from Dross Toll —and that this doubling and tripling of past and future, not to mention past and futures of other worlds, would cause a cataclysm we could not conceive.

"I remember the man, his pupils were like black discs. He was afraid. I do not know how he survived the poison that touched his mind, but we could see that the man was not lying. We, in our caverns above the ocean, met and decided that this anomaly deserved investigation. Because his tale reeked of magic, we decided that there would be few who were capable enough to defeat this threat but our own. We spoke and shared knowledge. Ideas, insights. And all the while, the man tossed and turned in wretched sleep. We came to the conclusion that with our dwindling numbers, it was not right to send more than one of us. We are keepers of knowledge, death worshiper. It is not right that we put the survival of our people in peril. So, it was decided that only one of us should go, to do whatever it takes to annihilate this distortion. That night I was chosen."

"And what of the man?" asked Corpse.

Jessa grimaced. "During our talks, he woke from his slumber and wandered the caves. He found an opening and he jumped. We found him on the rocks below, before the tide came in. His head was crushed like a rotten gourd, his innards dashed about the jagged points of the rocks. We could hold no funeral for this man; minutes after, his body was washed away to sea."

Corpse bowed his head and imagined getting sucked below the ocean's current, cold salt water filling his lungs. Suffocation. Desperation. Terror. And then, as he had heard others say, a creeping warmth that brought with it the end of consciousness. The story made his stomach twist, even as he envied the man brave enough to defeat self-preservation.

Jessa said, "Corpse, look at me."

Corpse was not accustomed to the bard using his name.

"Please, I beg of you. Take me to the tower."

The night was silent save for the crackling of wood.

He sighed. "Yes," he said. "Let's go."

12

WHAT COMES FROM DEATH

THE BALD WOMAN'S skin was covered in tattoo ink. She stood, imposing and dour, until her eyes caught a familiar sight. "Mirth," she said. But she did not smile or run or hug or make any exclamation. Instead, her dark eyes flickered with recognition and nothing more.

Mirth was serving a customer a flagon of ale when she heard her name. She was in such a haste to come to the woman, when the man offered her payment, she waved it away. "Not now, dear," she said. She seemed primed to hug the woman until she fully recognized the guest's stony nature. Keeping her arms straight to her side, she did her best to match her demeanor.

"You came," she said.

"You called."

"Thank you," said Mirth. "It's nice to see you after so long. Good Martyr, I've gotten old, Therin."

"Yes," she said. "But you are reckoning with it well, I take it?"

"As well as most."

Her severe lips formed a short pale slash across her face. "Have they found him yet?"

"There's been no word."

"They will not find him. Unless he lets them. And if they do, they will lose their lives."

Mirth asked, "Will you tell me who he is?"

"You will find out soon enough. First, take me to your Count Viniri."

"Yes, Therin," said Mirth, unsettled by her caustic demeanor. "Of course."

She caught Garrt smiling from the corner of her eye.

Therin stood by the door waiting, "I take it your Viniri resides in the castle? If you'd rather make eyes at your friend, I can find it myself."

Mirth nodded apologetically. But as she led Therin to the castle, she tightened her hands into fists.

* * *

THEY MARCHED ALL NIGHT, the smell of smoke in the air, gaining ground on the next infestation. I am scared, *he thought.* I should not be scared.

But he was. And there was little he could do but distract himself with the sights and sounds of the woods. He compared them to his home. Here, the trees were shorter, leafless. The bark was white. Fog hung low over flat, hard-packed earth. The wilderness was inhospitable. He shuddered at the thought of his body failing here, rotting in such a bleak landscape.

The others seemed similarly preoccupied, but enthusiastic. In between long drifting glances toward the opaque horizon, they would beat their chest and scream of blood and murder and release. True freedom. Corpse tried doing the same things, although he was not as good at it as them.

Night fell and General Loss had put her hand up in the air which told them it was time for them to be silent. They hushed and Corpse was alone with his thoughts, traveling on heavy feet with his blade drawn.

"I see them," said General Loss, whispering. She hunched over, her eyes like slits. "See? There?"

They all followed her gaze. Sure enough, in the illuminated fog, figures danced. Orange firelight bounced off the trees.

"Likely little more than a tribe," said Loss.

"Maybe just a family," said Corpse.

Loss turned to him. "And because they are blood, and together, shall we allow them to suffer?" Her voice brimmed with anguish, empathy.

"Of course not."

She leaned into his ear. "Free them, Corpse."

Her eyes sparkled in the moonlight. Corpse's heart pounded in his chest. He took a deep breath. "Yes, General," he said.

Corpse pulled out in front of Loss and motioned to the others. Three fingers in the air, with the thumb outstretched. Pay attention, look at me.

They knew Corpse well. They'd seen him fight. They'd seen him return soul after soul to the Earth's atomic garden. They trusted him.

Corpse stared into the fog. In truth, he was honored to take lead of Loss' army of proselytizers. It was a welcome distraction. "They have few, we have many...," he started. Then, a puzzle piece snapped into place.

Loss watched him with curiosity. "Tell us your orders, Corpse."

"My orders are to—my orders are to stand down. I will kill them alone."

"What?"

He took a step away from the others, separating himself from them. "Have I not killed more than any here? There are likely less than six, less than that are adults. Listen." Between the shadows, the sound of a child's laughter. "We can do more good with less sacrifice if I go alone."

General Loss rubbed her hands in the coolness of the night. Corpse braced for resistance.

But none came. "Save them," she said. "And after, find us west. Follow our trail of blood."

"Yes, General."

Loss motioned for the others to follow her. As they passed Corpse, they dourly saluted him. This was their eulogy.

The others disappeared into the fog. They were a silent bunch, their footsteps sounded as if they fell underwater. As soon as he was alone, he wished for them to be near. He had grown accustomed to them; to their swinging blades, and heavy hearts.

The silhouettes continued to dance. Corpse drew his blade, steeling himself. When he killed, the nervy energy that bounced around his soul dampened, diminishing into a lowly wail that could not be heard above the screams of his fallen.

He lightly stepped over roots, dreading each step, while staying in the shadows. The firelight grew brighter. It bloomed in the fog with orange light. It was pleasing.

Closer now, he heard laughter.

Closer now, he heard words.

Corpse hid behind a tree. It was only a family. A woman, a man, and a child. The woman played a lute and sang—her words drawn out tunefully, floating in and out of the fire's distorted aura.

"Away from the river, we carry our hearts into the hands of a grinning king! He gives us a taste of his mutton and wine and in his court we sing!"

The man and child danced. The man was squat with thick sideburns and glinting eyes. He hopped up and down like a frog, *whilst holding his daughter's hands. She giggled and he giggled too. They sang along with the woman, the father harmonizing when he could, although he did not share her vocal talent.*

Corpse studied them. They were pretending. They were fighting. He knew all about fighting. He'd seen plenty of it.

The song ended. The father lifted the girl by her armpits and hugged her tight. He kissed her on the forehead and then returned her lightly to the ground.

His heart beat a staggering rhythm. There is nothing left to do but release them. Or die here and now. Or or or—

Another thought came to him. Or rather—every decision he made thus far led him to put words to a feeling that had only been incoherent noise. What if I didn't?

A thousand thoughts bloomed like spring flowers in his mind. They opened their petals to him and he was at once in awe and in terror. He had thoughts, yes. He had many thoughts. He'd thought many thoughts over many years but none were like this. The same cold pessimism roiled within him, but it was now interlocked with something else.

The woman began another song. The man and child smiled.

He envied their good spirits.

And really, his thoughts at that moment were like a spinning coin. On one side was his blade, on the other was the unknown. Corpse sat with his discomfort.

But the coin kept spinning and spinning and each side had their words. Sometimes his sword would dip. Sometimes his grip would tighten. Once, he nearly turned his back to the family. He was ready to walk away, to run into the blackness of the woods. He could lie to Loss. Or he could fall on his sword now, yards away from the singing family. But that coin kept spinning. And the battle grew slower, bloodier. It wobbled. It fell.

And he wasn't thinking, not really. Corpse didn't have to. It was muscle memory. Three targets—he would make a fine braggart.

The woman closed her eyes when she sang. She didn't see Corpse emerge from the wall of blackness.

The father and daughter danced in a circle and they didn't see him either—at first.

One circle. Two circles. Three circles. Then—

The girl's eyes widened. Two moons. "Who is th—?"

Corpse swung the blade and her mother's head rolled onto the earth, her instrument fell to the ground. The man was slow to react. He danced. He turned to his daughter, asking "Honey, what?" But a scream was already on her throat. Shrill, piercing. Corpse's heart hurt. Because there was nothing scarier than being alive.

The man then turned to his headless wife and the ghostly form that loomed over her. He shared eyes with his daughter. Two moons.

The fire separated them.

"Who are you?"

He did not answer.

The man backed away, pulling his daughter close to him. "You can let us go. We haven't done anything. You can take everything we have." His voice wavered. "Just let us live."

Corpse shook his head. "I can't do that."

"Yes, you can!"

The girl's large eyes peered out from behind the father. They locked in on her mother, dead on the hard earth.

Corpse pitied her. He threw his sword like a spear, so fast that neither of them could let out a gasp when the blade pierced through the girl's center, sending her toppling over. She laid on the ground, blood mixing in the dancing shadows.

It happened so fast, it took the father a moment to process the sudden violence. He looked down at the girl and then to

Corpse. Slowly, it dawned on him. An inhuman noise emerged from his throat.

The father fell to his knees, he took her head and cradled it close to his chest. Globules of tears slid down his cheeks, mucus ran from his nose, and he pushed his face deep into his child's hair, breathing in her scent a final time. He hugged her, crushed her, as if he were seeking to save her by making her part of him.

Corpse had only his hands now but he had killed many with them. He approached the man, who was now little more than a puddle, just like his daughter. There would be no chase.

The man sobbed. His throat was raw and his crying became so miserably acute that he was now coughing in between them. "Lianay," he whispered. "Lianay, Lianay."

It would be quick.

Corpse was now close enough to touch the man. He reached down to touch his head.

The man wailed into the night. "No," he blubbered. "No!" He scrambled backward, dragging his daughter's body with him. "Get away! Leave us!"

Corpse followed him. The man was not fast. He kept pulling his daughter closer to him, as if keeping her near would somehow ward the reaper off. As if people only die when they're alone.

"It'll be quick," he said, a sense of pleading in his voice. "Just stay still."

The man spat between his tears. "Fuck off, devil! You've— you've—" He hugged the dead girl tighter. Her skin had become pale, her blood covered him. Corpse thought, in a way, that he looked dead already.

The man breathed heavily, his chest rising up and down and his daughter rising with it, her mask-like face pressed against his chest. He hung his head next to her ear and said, "Please, please,

please. Leave me be. Just leave me be. Just leave me alone." A sob. "I don't want to die."

Corpse kneeled and pulled the blade from the girl. The man reacted with a start, a tremor, as if the blade had been pulled from his own intestines. He slumped over, cradling her, calling out her name, falling over in the fetal position.

He did not want to die.

On the edges of the firelight, Corpse felt ill. Wrong. Uncanny. Strange. The man did not want to die. He was not lying. Because, why would he? It was the worst day of his life, surely. His pain was horrible. And yet, he begged for his life. Begged.

His daughter's body muffled his screams.

Corpse disappeared, back into the night. He hoped that his peers could not hear the man's wails.

* * *

THIS ISN'T RIGHT, thought Placate.

But then again, what was right?

Warmth crept into her body. Her skin burned to the touch. Visions blossomed in her mind.

Horrible, terrifying visions. Glimpses of worlds she was never meant to see. Of timelines under duress. Extinction given form and function. *The Martyr was right.*

Religious joy welled in her heart as the tower beckoned her closer, pulling her *into* it. She'd always wanted to be a part of something bigger. That's why she was so keen to be one of the Count's guards. But, of course, even that was lacking compared to this.

A slit appeared in its skin, taller than her, and red spilled out. Her body screamed for her to go inside, to crawl into that warm open gash, to wallow.

She reached out, she gave in to her body's scream.

It felt good, as if a great dissonance had been resolved. One that she never knew existed.

Inside it, she felt like she was floating in a great sea of birthing fluid.

A voice whispered to her, only one word, but it rang in her ears, it burned into her brain, it echoed within her bones.

SPREAD.

A slit opened again, burning with sumptuous light. She almost didn't want to leave but the tower pushed her. It told her everything she needed to hear to leave and feel strong, feel good.

She forgot why she came here in the first place. Everything looked red.

As the cool air hit her, adrenaline coursed through her veins. She felt stronger, imbued with a gift—a tumor, an infection—and a wild urge to share it.

She ran back through the woods to the others. She could smell regret, boredom. They had stopped believing.

"The young traveler returns," said La'Dir. "Welco— Placate, what's wrong with your eyes?"

The other men turned to her, their curious expressions turning to disgust in seconds. "Why are you wet? What's wrong?"

Placate bared sharp teeth. Her red eyes blazed under the indigo sky.

The men held their weapons tight.

* * *

SCREAMS.

Corpse and Jessa held still.

"There is something amiss," said the bard.

He had heard many types of screams before. These were screams of agony. His fingers curled around the edges of a tree whilst searching the darkness for some sense of the threat.

"This is not good," said Corpse. "I do not want to die."

"No man wants to die," said Jessa. "That is the nature of being alive."

"It is a terrible nature."

"It is all we know." He was silent for a moment, then: "I will likely die tonight."

Corpse searched his eyes for truth. "It will take that much magic then to defeat this thing?"

Jessa nodded solemnly. "It will, yes."

"Can I ask you something?"

"Yes."

"Are you frightened?"

"Of course." Jessa placed a hand on Corpse's back. A gentle touch. He said nothing more.

Corpse's eyes welled in the darkness of the forest as another scream sounded. He blinked, clearing his throat. "We should hurry," he said.

* * *

La'Dir swung his broadsword in wide arcs to scare off the girl with red eyes and dozens of shark-like teeth. "Get away from me, demon!"

She approached him with a single-minded menace.

Behind her, he could see the others rising by moonlight, their eyes glowing red in the dark of the forest.

Just being near her made his head throb and ache. He felt as if his mind had been colonized by her memories.

They invaded him, filled him with horrific images. They told stories of great reptilian gods and unraveling spools of time; irate devils and exploding suns. They slipped in and out of his head with remarkable ease.

In a matter of seconds, the girl had been stabbed, bludgeoned, and stomped on. When she lunged toward the first guard, he ran her through.

But that was not enough. The wound bled freely, *but she did not die.*

A spear pierced her heart. La'Dir thought surely that would kill her; Placate gasped, as if something had been taken from her. But again: no. She continued on.

She killed the first man by tearing his head off. She made it seem like a simple matter. Her fingers worked themselves into his flesh, then deeper to the bone, and with one quick yank the head went flying atop a geyser of red blood.

La'Dir and the others backed away, their mouths agape.

It didn't take long before the girl tore through the others too. Each person she killed was taken by her blood. Around her a faint red miasma hung in the air. Each of the bodies she damned to hell stood right back up after they were slain, blinking the same red-pink eyes in the black of the night.

La'Dir feinted with the tip of his blade. Only enough to push her back a step. Placate snarled. Gore covered her from head-to-toe—bits of herself and her fallen comrades.

La'Dir had seen many battles before. He had killed many men; he had served under Count Viniri for decades. There was no man born and bred of Dross Toll that was a better swordsman. But, La'Dir was accustomed to killing *people.*

Swoosh, swoosh.

He kept the sword moving, stepping backward. The bloodied horde approached with cracked eyes and hungry mouths.

Swoosh, swoosh.

Back again.

La'Dir tried to assemble a plan. He had known some of these guards for years. Others had been here as long as he. Was the girl a witch of some sort? A foreign interest bent on destabilizing Dross Toll?

Swoosh, swoosh.

Perhaps the Count was right. Perhaps the Count was right more than he gave him credit for.

The girl stopped. "Fester and rot," she said, her voice scraping like steel on bone. "Are you ready to join your soldiers, Captain?"

Swoosh, swoosh.

As he saw the glimmer of a feral sadism flash across Placate's eyes, he turned sharply—dropping his sword (*useless*, he thought), and running, throwing himself through the woods in the dark. There was no light under the canopy. Only a faint glow of red. He ran and ran and ran and behind him the ragged voices of a hellish brood followed.

13
MADNESS

Count Viniri wore robes of red. His long fingers hooked gold rings hanging from his belt in tense but idle play.

Three knocks at the door. He held his breath. *Hopefully La'Dir has returned*, he thought.

"Come in."

A servant cracked the door open, bowing, then said, "A woman is here to see you. Two women, in fact."

"I don't have time for commoners today."

"This isn't a commoner. It's the lady from the inn, Mirth. She comes with a foreigner."

"Tell her we've had our fill." He cast a cruel glance toward the servant who appropriately withered.

"Well, sir," said the servant. "I—"

Viniri sneered. The servant would die, he decided. *How dare—*

"The woman is from the Malwoods, sire. She has information on the man. The one who...." His words trailed off.

Viniri licked his teeth under his lips as the servant stared at the floor, no doubt frozen in fear. Finally, the Count said, "Yes, bring her in."

When he returned, Viniri swallowed his disgust at the foreign woman with the tattooed skin, just as he feigned magnanimous joy at the presence of Mirth, who made no similar pretensions. Viniri was not used to the people of Dross Toll meeting his gaze.

"Mirth, it's been too long," he said.

"It's been long enough, Count. I'm only here to deliver the words of a friend. You arrested a boarder of mine, one who I believe is innocent. You and your guards were foolish and paid dearly for it. Therin is here to help so that you don't pay with your life."

The Count laughed. "Please, sit down. Yes, let's have wine. Food? Can I interest you in food?"

Therin shook her head.

"So, I take it from your strange appearance that you are one of those fearsome warrior-priests from the Malwoods I've heard so much about. A friend of the man named Corpse?"

"Not a friend," she bristled. "But a peer."

"A peer?" He scoffed. "This is already growing irritating. Say what you came to say or get out."

"In the Malwoods, we have a saying: the greatest curse to befall man is dying, the second is living." Her words came out like an icy wind. "I'm more traveled than most, so I understand how others must think of us."

"So, you're saying you know what happens in the mind of a royal now? Lovely meeting you but perhaps it's best if you fuck off back to where you came from."

"I've come this far," said Therin. "I'll deliver my message. You can do with it what you will. Corpse was a boy raised in a culture of death—just like myself. You will never be able to understand our relationship with our own demise. We both welcome and abhor it. It is a sickness within us constantly. Most of us die early by our own hands. Some of us take control of death by inviting it, by going to war. By wiping out townships and relieving others of the same burden."

"Barbarians," spat the Count.

"Yes, that's what you call us. And do you know what we call you?" She waited. When the Count said nothing, her lips curled around a single word: "Corpses."

"My men are out in the woods right now and they'll be bringing him back any moment. Perhaps you should stay. You can watch your Corpse embrace his namesake."

"How many men did you send?"

The Count paused, his eternally cocked eyebrows now reaching halfway up his forehead. He looked as if he had not expected to seriously consider the question. Finally, he said, "Fifteen, maybe. More or less."

"They're dead now."

Viniri laughed. "Such ego. You think one man has any chance against a dozen of my guards?"

"First fifteen, now twelve," said Therin. "What next? Ten? The fact of the matter, *Count,* is that I don't think anything when it comes to Corpse. I *know.* And if you had done your due diligence, you would too."

"Careful with those accusations," said the Count coldly. "You are in my castle. I did nothing to insult your tribesman."

"You've treated him fairly then?"

"He killed one of my guards," Viniri growled.

"Your guard was killed by magic. Our people do not practice sorcery. Your men were too eager to flex their meager authority. And without my help, you'll pay for it."

Count Viniri considered this in silence. "And why is it that you want to help me?"

"I have my reasons," said Therin. "Corpse is a capable priest but we do not care if he dies. We do care, however, if he does not. You need my help. Your guards are already rotting."

"You insult me in my own court!"

Mirth, who had been silent so far, looked to Therin, a curious expression of distrust and sorrow.

"I can have you punished. I can have you *killed*, do you understand?"

"You can not kill me," said Therin. "Your bones are brittle and your mind jumps at shadows. I can kill Corpse. All you have to do is let us go unbothered, then we'll both be out of Dross Toll, and you can continue your reign of incompetence unfettered."

His cheeks went red. "I will have your h—"

But before he could fully declare his vengeance, a knock rang out from the door.

"Not now!" he called.

The door opened a crack. A servant's hand trembled on the jamb.

"Can you not hear?" said Viniri with maximum venom.

"It's Captain La'Dir," he said.

Viniri's face contorted in triumph. "Oh, it seems my dear friend has returned with the head of the man named Corpse!"

The servant shook his head. "No," he said. "He comes alone. And not well. He wishes to speak to you."

"I'll be waiting," said Therin.

She turned around, Mirth following her, and as the door closed behind them, they heard a wretched scream. Therin laughed, the sound of bones in a tin cup.

"Corpse is a good man," said Mirth quietly. "He doesn't deserve this."

"We deserve what we get."

Outside the castle, the roar of chaos sounded. Men on cats patrolled the outer walls. Therin quickened her pace and Mirth did her best to keep up.

14

VINIRI'S FINEST

Corpse's blade sliced clean through one of the red-eyed bastards. A diagonal cut, from hip to shoulder. He screamed, bleeding violently, before splitting in two.

When they saw the crowd of soldiers, blood-slicked and running, Corpse told Jessa to hide.

The bard scurried up a tree and suddenly Corpse was alone with the small horde of guards, and without a second of hesitation, he swung.

From above, Jessa said, "Kill them quickly, if you—"

But Corpse could not hear him over the clashing of blades.

A spear thrusted toward him, but Corpse jumped back so that it only grazed at his clothes. He grabbed the shaft of the weapon and pulled it forward, holding his own sword straight out. The guard, in his venomous bloodlust, did not think to let go of the shaft, wrestling it with bloody white knuckles. He jerked forward, following Corpse's pull, right into his outstretched blade.

Corpse kicked him off, leaving a trail of black blood in the moonlight.

A dark shape fell over him, sending him crashing into the dense underbrush, losing his sword in the scuffle. He rolled several times, flicking up rocks, tasting dirt, and being punched by large roots—all the while the thing scratched at him like a feral beast.

He righted himself, flipping over to see the red-eyed devil that had her hands on his neck.

She was strong. Stronger than she had any right to be. As she pressed down on his throat, her gaze became implacably content.

He tried to cough. A soft puff of air died somewhere in his esophagus as he struggled back and forth.

"*Jessa!*" The words came out in a whisper.

How was she so strong?

Behind her, more of the Red Guards gathered—their lips drawn in violent hunger. Corpse searched his attacker for a weapon, a dagger, perhaps. Something small and tucked into her belt that he could grab and slash across her throat. Nothing.

The sound of his own blood rushed in his ears. He looked up into those red eyes and saw the vastness of other worlds swirling within them.

Perhaps it won't be so bad, he thought. *Perhaps this is the moment I've spent my whole life waiting for.*

Warmness kissed his extremities. A lackadaisical sense of belonging came over him. He wondered if this is how everyone else felt.

But the warmness ceased and the euphoria escalated into neuroses. The dark came calling for him, claiming him with its dark claws and he did not feel that he was dying anymore, but rather that he was being taken. His body was to be destroyed and visions of the Two-Headed Martyr—a god he did not even believe in—swarmed his head. As the paranoid darkness closed its maw around his thoughts, which had become nothing more than a pinprick of light in a darkness so loud and large it defied comprehension, as the frigid cold arrested him, he thought with dread on what world's future or past he'd wake up to.

The woman's hands released him.

He gasped.

Warmth.

Real warmth.

He blinked. He breathed.

He heard her land somewhere beyond the others. They turned their heads to see her pass but it was too dark and she was too fast for Corpse to see.

"Get up, death worshiper! Now! Get up!"

Jessa shook him by the shoulder. He took Corpse's hand and squeezed it around his sword.

"Oh," he said, dazed, "You've found my weapon."

"Yes, now get up. I can't fight them. I will die if I have to fight them. Hurry now. Up!"

Corpse sat up. The air felt good in his lungs. The remaining guards marched toward him, only a dozen feet away.

"Up, damn you!"

Corpse stood. He held out his sword, on unsteady feet. He said to Jessa, "I almost died."

"Yes, I know. But please!"

He wobbled slightly.

The guard at the front of the formation raised his sword.

"Yes," said Corpse.

Silver clashed in the night. But even in his near-death

haze, the stranger from the Malwoods easily dispatched the guard with a single slice across his belly. The guard howled as his entrails spilled out in a steaming pile.

"Good," yelled Jessa. "Good! Get me to the tower and we can end this madness!"

Corpse sliced and gutted enemy after enemy. He kicked a guard against a tree and muscled his blade through the space within his screaming mouth. The top half of his head fell to the ground. He hooked the blade underneath a man's spine—a deathly wound itself—then sliced it free. The guard clawed feebly on jellied legs as Corpse's coup de gras removed his head. Others took a modicum of more time, a drop more of skill. One guard threw a spear that Corpse deflected easily with his sword, but only as a distraction. In the moment it took Corpse to block the shaft and throw it aside, the guard had lunged toward him with a short sword that looked as sharp as a viper's fang. Corpse dropped to his knees, just low enough for the edge to miss his head by a hair; he thrust the blade up through the guard's stomach and pulled it out through the side, as entrails rained wetly onto the forest floor.

He cut through all of them. He bestowed his namesake upon the red-eyed soldiers. When he stood in the center of their bleeding bodies and dead eyes, they were no longer men, only corpses.

Jessa came back from his hiding space, his face somber. Perhaps it was the electric buzz in the air. The encroachment of one world on another.

The air *squirmed.*

Corpse looked to Jessa for an explanation, but the bard wore nothing on his face but abject horror.

The ferns rustled. The underbrush shook. Organs and

limbs and decapitated heads slithered on living blood and found their homes. Wounds resealed with the wet kiss of magic.

And the Count's guards stood again, their lips pulled back to reveal sharp, yellow teeth.

15
"MORE!"

Captain La'Dir was in no *physical* pain when they brought him to the castle, a fact that only served to make his Count more wickedly cruel.

"Perhaps I should stab you now, old friend. To make up for what you obviously missed in battle."

The captain took his glancing blows as he waited for his turn to explain.

"And how did this child overpower you?"

"I can't say, sire. She killed the other guards in minutes. She tore through them."

Viniri rolled his eyes. "Yes, she tore through them and these guards, now in bits and pieces, stood up. They're mincemeat, you fucking idiot!" He could barely contain his anger anymore.

But Captain La'Dir stayed true to his story. "I don't know how it happened, but it did. There is magic in those woods. And it's not a kind magic. Your Corpse might be looking for it. Either way, he's dead now. I passed him on the way back. I was being chased. They saw him and I think I lost them in the trees."

Viniri grinded his teeth. "Are you trying to make a fool of me, La'Dir?"

He shook his head. "No, no. Of course not, sire! I would never! I speak the truth!"

"A woman came here," said the Count. "Mirth, the barkeep, came with her. She says she used to know this Corpse."

"Oh?"

"Yes. She wants to bring him back with her, she called me foolish. Can you believe that? This is my reputation, La'Dir. Even as far as the Malwoods go, I am now known as an incompetent ruler. Do you understand why that makes me so angry? And now, I find out that you came back to me, with nary a scratch on you. You return from the forest, not with Corpse's head, but with ghost stories. How do you think that makes me look?"

He approached an ancient bureau, opening a drawer.

"Sire," said La'Dir. "There are larger problems than your ego." The words slipped from his mouth so quickly that he wasn't sure he said them aloud at first. He continued, "Corpse has no interest in killing you and is incapable of single-handedly destroying Dross Toll. He is on the run. But those *things* out there are not. They gave me a dream of their sickness. I can see like the Martyr did. Two worlds happening at once, colliding." He buried his face into his hands. "They wish to spread their sickness. Forget Corpse, I beg of you. Kill the sickness that lives in the woods."

Viniri held an artifact close to his sides. He shook his head slowly. "Poor, La'Dir. You have failed me. But I will heed your request. Servant!" he called. "Gather fifty of our troops and send them into the woods to track our missing soldiers, and kill them."

"Yes, sire."

"And tell them to bring back Corpse's head as well."

"Yes, sire."

"Now, La'Dir, we have another matter to attend to. I have sent more guards into the forest and they will surely be able to kill a man with ease. Fifty men to do what ten could not." Viniri uncoiled a whip, letting its serpentine body fall to the floor. "But there must be punishment too for failure."

La'Dir bowed his head, shaking it back and forth. "Please, sire."

"Yes," said Viniri, whose eyes were now alight. "There are people here who believe I did not earn this throne. Mirth and her father, for two. But power is not something we're born into, it is a thing we seize. You have heard the rumors of my magic, yes?"

"Yes," said La'Dir. He backed away. The rumors of Viniri's magical prowess were an open secret, a folktale whispered between thieves and political enemies. The Count never confirmed or denied his fascination with the occult, only offering a sardonic smile at the implication.

"*C'tha l'adirra,*" he said and La'Dir felt his body seize up. His eyes swirled in frozen sockets. Viniri came ever closer to him. "You may not be familiar with the root of your name, La'Dir. Not everyone is. It comes from the old tongue. One not spoken since the time of the Martyr—Drosleté. It was said to be a language that could move worlds and that's precisely why it fell out of favor. Imagine that, language being a dangerous thing. Of course, when the early residents of Dross Toll decided to bury their own language, not all of them agreed. Some of the *oldest* blood kept Drosleté as a family secret, a tradition. For my family, it was a religion, nearly. For yours, it was but trivia. A vulgar remembrance of the old ways. Paid homage to in your name, which is a bastardization of *l'adirra*, devoid of anything but the most fleeting power. Your name, La'Dir, refers to the chasm of twilight. A spiritual place between living and dead. Do you know what mine means?"

La'Dir felt deep terror shiver through his body, although he could not show it. Inside of him, his heart pounded on the bones of his ribcage.

"*Viniri*, in its original Drosleté, translates roughly to: a blossom of pain. A juxtaposition of beauty and torture." The Count held the whip up, whispering to it as it began to take a life of its own, twisting and hissing on the floor. To La'Dir's horror, the end of the whip opened into the fanged smile of a slit-pupiled adder.

Viniri cracked the whip.

"Viniri and La'Dir. The blossom of pain meets the chasm of twilight. There is poetry to that, yes?"

La'Dir focused desperately, tears emerging from the corners of his eyes, to make his mind go blank.

Viniri said, "Goodbye, old friend."

His feet did not allow him to rejoin his brethren. They kept him still, planting him between fallen logs covered in fine, glassy moss.

I could go home, perhaps.

He had a grave there. Maybe Loss was right. Maybe she knew it was his time before he did. Corpse imagined his return. Would it be celebratory? Somber? Would old friends with whom he had shared drink, sorrow, and his innermost soul welcome him back? Would they take him by the hand with envy and solidarity and trust and kindness and let him take his place amongst the earth that held his parents and the souls that came before him? Would the earth feel cold to his touch, or would it be an embrace? Would his grave hug him like the father squeezed his daughter?

Morning light came. He waited longer still.

Embarrassment, another of life's insults.

When he was sure that he would not cross paths with his former battalion, he stood and began his journey. It was decided. He would go home to die.

16

THE AWFUL TRUTH

Therin went to bed immediately on her arrival, saying no parting words to Mirth or Garrt. Her friend's vanishing brought her a moment of comfort, a reprieve.

She laid her head on the bar and wondered silently if calling on her was a good idea at all.

Garrt poured two glasses of ale and placed one in front of Mirth. The tavern was closed, the guests were in bed. The two drank by the dwindling light of two half-burnt candles.

"Your friend giving you trouble?"

Mirth rubbed her temples. "It's been a troublesome day. She pushes our dear Count."

"An easy task, to be sure."

"I'm no stranger to it. We all know about the clashes he had with my father. The Count sees me as an elderly brat. I have tested his limits, used what small resources I've had to make good on both of my inheritances: gold and a father's hate."

"It was earned though, was it not?"

"Yes," said Mirth, "I believe it was." She stared down

into the brown foamy liquid. "I met Therin not long after the Count murdered my father for false treason."

"You had left Dross Toll," he said. "I remember."

"Yes, I did. I was young once. Do you remember me as I was, when I was young? Or do you think of me now, now that I am old?"

"I see you as all of those and more, bless the Martyr. I am only a score younger than you, Mirth. Let's not pretend that we're so different. You cradled me as a child, yes. But we also drank together, laughed, and occasionally loved. I see you as a friend."

She touched his hand. "It's hard to grow old. But it is true, you are a friend. I've been lucky to have many friends in my lifetime. Therin, I suppose, is one of the stranger ones."

"Where did you meet her? In the Malwoods?"

"No, no," she said. "But near. Over in Valant, the Shared City."

"I have heard of Valant. It is, supposedly, quite a sight."

"It is," said Mirth. "Beautiful. It is a lovely city that takes in all sorts. People from many different cultures gather there and settle. Some of the nearby tribes also come in to do business, or for earthly pleasures. There is much to be had in Valant—drink, love, good food, gambling. It is a hedonist's paradise, but it is also a kind place."

"I should hope to visit one day. I've only heard stories."

"You should. When this episode concludes, we can close the inn and I'll take you. I met Therin when she was barely of age, a cruel but curious fourteen year old. That was over thirty years ago." She shook her head. "Maybe I wasn't so young at the time. Only younger than I am now."

"Aye." He lifted his glass.

"I was reading in the square when I saw this young girl who looked unlike anyone I'd ever seen. Her hair was short, tattoos covered her skull. Her eyes were black and serious. I'd never seen a child who appeared so wisened beyond her years. She stomped around Valant's square, clearly seeking some sort of trouble. She found the first guard she saw and pulled a rapier on him. My mouth dropped. This strange child had just pierced the man's stomach. When he fell dead, she waited for his counterparts to appear. 'Come now!' she yelled. 'Come now and test your mettle against me!' It was a braggadocios call, at least superficially, but her voice trembled. The guard on the ground squirmed, cursing at her. Dying, but slowly. Guards came running and Therin, just a girl, stood with her thin blade pointed outward with a grimace on her lips."

Garrt nodded. "She wanted to die."

"Yes," said Mirth. "She did. She had come to Valant to die in battle. For them, it's often the easiest way to pass."

"What happened?"

"The guards were slow to arrive. Every second a lifetime. There I was, sitting by a fountain, reading fanciful fantasies, and the next I was watching this child try to get herself killed. I had no children and I wanted none—that has always been true, old friend—but I felt a draw toward her, an urge to protect, even just for a moment. So, after only a couple of moments, I stood up and went to her quickly, while the other Valantians covered their mouths and held their breath. They are a strange type there, predisposed to passivity. The only world they know is their own. When I realized that, I also realized that I was never meant to be one of them.

"Therin pointed her sword at me. She told me that if I

interfered with her, I would die. And I told her that if I did not, she would as well. I saw in her eyes that this mattered little to her, that she was sprinting to her own grave, here and now. I told her that there are better ways out than this. That there was no use in killing anyone. That the man did not need to die, and neither did she."

Garrt sighed. "But why fight with her? She was a murderer, was she not?"

"Yes, she was. But she was also a girl. A child. Men like Viniri would put children in dungeons for their foibles. And you know what my father said about those who swear to uphold laws, 'the only man who should not be trusted to police others is the man that wants to.' I did not care that much about the guard, for better or worse. If he had not died there, he would die somewhere else. Perhaps from an angry drunk not ready to close his tab. Being killed by a child was a better way to go than most are afforded."

"You did not tell young Therin this."

"No, I did not." Mirth laughed. "I was wise enough to keep my own opinions to myself that day. Instead, I told her to come with me for three days, that we could go anywhere we wanted and eat anything we desired. For those three days, we could be free from whatever duties fell on our shoulders, and after, if she wanted to resume this violence, I would not stop her."

"And she said?"

"I swear her eyes widened and I saw the child beneath the despair. She was not a monster. A whisper of a tear pooled in the corners of her eyes and as we heard the faraway howls of the guards get ever closer, she gave me a curt nod and went with me. I had a cat tied nearby and by the time the guards arrived, we were already galloping down the streets to the city limits."

"You have lived a full life, Mirth. Fuller than most can claim."

"Aye," she said, smiling wanly. "The guilt sometimes makes me feel as if I have no business waging my petty wars with Viniri. That I have more in common with him than the folk I defend, feed, and hide when they need it. But alas."

"What happened with you and the girl?"

"Therin and I rode out of Valant with not a single warrior in pursuit. We left as if we were never there to begin with. The next three days we stayed in the small mountain city of Bounty Cane. We stayed in a hotel and ate, saw plays, and amused ourselves. I won't be so proud to say that I changed Therin forever, but for three days she was less a warrior and more of a child. Even for a couple of days, it was good to distract her. To remind her that there was life beyond her own melancholy. At the end of the three days, she thanked me and told me she must be going home. She told me how to write to her and I told her how to reach me as well. And then, she was gone. In another two years, I heard back from this strange girl and we became correspondents. We shared our lives with each other, and I suppose having had that shared with me, I should have known..." She motioned to the ceiling above her. "...that a modicum of care was not enough to change an entire culture."

Garrt stuck his lower lip out, thinking. "It is a strange thing, how we are raised. They are shackles we cannot break."

"If we cannot, I do not want to know. I need to believe otherwise."

The candles burned all the way down to nothing and Garrt extinguished them with his thumb and forefinger.

The tavern went black, except for the faint glow of moonlight that dripped in through the windows. "Let's finish our drinks in the dark," said Garrt. "I suppose it seems appropriate."

17

THE REFUSAL
OF THE REAPER

THE RED-EYED GUARDS were stitched together with sinew. Thin lines of fresh scar tissue wove itself in the pattern through which Corpse's sword had carved. The Malwoodsian and the bard stood tight together as the dead reformed.

"They do not die," said Jessa.

Corpse said, his voice full of woe, "They do not die *yet*." He raised his sword. "Your people read far and wide, yes?"

"I do not think words, even the Old Ones, will save us now."

"Have you heard of creatures like these?"

A guard whose head had only just reconnected, tested his misaligned vocal cords with a gurgle.

"Revenants? Yes. None have been seen in the flesh for a thousand years though."

"Can they be stopped?"

The reassembled guards flexed their own fingers, allowing their muscles to bulge.

"How do we kill them, Jessa?"

Jessa furrowed his brow, no doubt trying to recall

ancient, forgotten lore. "You could dismember them fully, perhaps. Destroy their heads. Burn them, maybe. There may also be a magical means, but I do not know it."

"A flame, then. You can conjure us one, yes?"

"No, I have not much time left if I am to destroy the tower. I need every minute."

The guards had gathered their weapons, their staggering had become smoother, more purposeful. "If I fought them now, you would be able to destroy the tower, yes?"

Jessa nodded.

"Okay, then," he said. "Go."

"What? You need my help."

"Go," said Corpse, his blade black and sharp in the moonlight. "I have waited all my life to die."

"Thank you, death worshiper," said Jessa. "I wish you well." He disappeared into the trees.

The guards let out a series of sharp, short grunts in a new language Corpse did not recognize.

His sword fell for just a moment. He saw their own blades and wondered if it were a language he too could learn. Better still, he wondered if that meant that there was language after death. If there were words in death, what else could there be?

The woman with the spear lunged after him. He swung his sword and sliced the spear's shaft, cutting it in two with a single blow. The dead guard's face went slack, but before she could react, Corpse buried the blade of his weapon deep into her skull.

The other revenants let out a fearful gasp. He pulled the blade out and then beheaded her. On the ground, he separated her torso from her legs. Then, again, he cut off her hands and her arms and her feet.

The magic did not die in her eyes.

But fear spiraled around her cracked pupils.

The other revenants stood by no longer.

Corpse held his bloody sword high. "Come to me now!" he cried. "Bring me to my grave!"

They all attacked at once, their mouths opened in hungry rage. Swords slashed in the night and as the night became dawn, they continued their battle.

The revenants proved to be a fierce opponent, they attacked with fervor akin to zealotry. They attacked him on all sides, but Corpse parried each of them, ducking and dodging spears as a pink dawn oozed across the sky.

Locked in combat, he stared one of the beasts in the eye, ready to muscle his blade into the revenant's throat.

Only—

He felt one of them launch into his flank. Not a weapon this time, but a body.

The air left him. He gasped.

Above him, the wild-eyed guard whose head was only just a little off, attempted to dig his teeth into his flesh.

If he tastes my flesh, I may never die, he thought.

He rolled down a slope, hitting tree trunks along the way.

Corpse tried to throw the guard off of him, but he latched on tight. His hand was on his throat, holding him just barely a foot away from his face. The guard's breath stank of an alien disease.

UGH!

This tree was wide, strong. Corpse crunched into it, feeling the pain in his ribs. He couldn't tell if it were his bones cracking or the twigs underneath him. In slow motion, he saw the guard lift off of him in the air, twirling like a dead leaf.

With empty hands, Corpse searched for a weapon. The

guards had begun their descent and the wild-eyed demon that tackled him was clawing through saplings to reach him again.

Corpse felt a sharp pain whenever he breathed, a dagger that drew blood with his moving chest. He held his side. He had heard stories of fighters who did not mind pain, who relished it, and he always felt a tinge of sadness that he would never be one of them. Those from the Malwoods felt pain very well. It was one of many excruciating elements of living that they abhorred.

The guard shambled toward him, all dirty fingers and crooked teeth. He realized then that its language was *pain* itself.

Corpse closed his eyes at the pink glow of sunrise. He swallowed his hurt as he launched himself into the air. Below him, the revenant craned its head to look up. Corpse felt as if he were flying.

And then, he brought his feet down on the thing's back. *Snap.*

Pain screamed through his side, as soon as he landed the hit, he bent over and stumbled off of the guard, holding his side as tears welled in his eyes.

The thing on the ground whimpered, but did not die.

Corpse regained his composure, seeing through the red of his pain, as guards slid down the hill on quick feet.

It would not take long for the guard's spine to heal.

Corpse looked around for something, anything.

Would the tower's death lead to the death of these things also?

He hoped Jessa had found it, was close to ending it. These opponents, in death, were more fierce than they had ever been in life.

Corpse dipped low to gather a large rock, a jagged stone

covered in moss. He heaved it up, adjusting his stance to hold it. It was so heavy that the dagger in his side gained inches with every breath.

The guard's spine cracked. The thing let out a warbling cry. It was healing. Its bones were snapping back into place with an unsteady organic rhythm.

Corpse let go of the rock, letting it fall from his hands, right onto the guards' head.

Black blood and brain matter exploded from the thing's skull, its limbs continued to jerk but it could not lift itself from the rock. Its head caved in—a flat sheet of brain matter pulverized into the forest floor.

Corpse did not wait to see if it too would reform, for the other guards had followed him, they raised their weapons and prepared to gut him but *the pain was already too much.* Corpse held his side, leaning against a tree for support.

He thought he might be dying. Each breath brought a burst of agony. His vision blurred.

Jessa, are you close? Jessa, what has happened?

Behind him, there was a roar.

He thought at first that it might be a loose cat.

(A blade came down and he stumbled to the side, its nicked blade notching itself into the tree.)

But the roar was not that of a cat. It was too large, too infernal. It was not just one thing. It was many.

(Corpse fell to the ground, rolling as a spear traveled through the air. When he stood, he held his side and grit his teeth, tears streaming down his cheeks.)

There were more of them. There were a lot more.

He could hear them.

Revenants?

He listened closer.

No.

He saw the first of them.

A sword thrust toward him. He felt the thick, flat blade cut through his skin, the hot blood spill out from his wound.

Corpse screamed but the ghoulish guard cackled and went to swing again. The eyes of the beast were foul. Unholy. The rest came to him, eager to take his blood. They would drench the earth with his insides.

There were more of them though. Those unlike these twisted beings. Men and women who wore swords and armor but had not yet been perverted by the tower.

As he dodged blows on shaking legs, he thought: *The Count has sent more guards.*

He caught the arm of one of them and twisted the broadsword from his wrist. He was armed now, but no better for wear. Under the dark canopy of unforgiving trees, death tugged at his psyche, ushering him back to the earth.

* * *

The tower stood tall, it breathed lightly. As if it did not know, nor wish to know, anything. It existed and nothing else.

Before it, stood a man.

18

THE RETURN

Garrt had begun the cooking—a large meal of poached eggs, roasted potatoes, and honeyed meats. The smell of it permeated the whole of the Drunken Prophet. Mirth often thought of Garrt's cooking as the surest way to rouse their boarders from their rooms.

But Therin did not come with the other weary travelers.

Mirth figured, at first, that she might be tired. She had traveled a long way, after all. And while Mirth knew more about those from the Malwoods than most in Dross Toll, their culture was still a mystery to her. *Perhaps it is her custom to sleep late.*

But a part of her knew, when she knocked, that Therin would not be present.

Mirth opened her door with weary resignation.

The bed was made. No items were left behind.

The room was bare. And just as she suspected, Therin was gone.

** * **

Viniri chose his new captain with the same care that he chose his meals. He asked who was available, and then asked how good they were. When those matters were settled, he selected Kirka Rust—a valiant fighter and home-grown resident of Dross Toll with more than ten years experience in the Count's guard.

Kirka, in turn, accepted the job as she did any other—with a nod and a polite affirmation.

Kirka left the Count's hall and within the hour her barely suppressed rage now found its outlet on the back of a riding cat, where she screamed her war cry with a small army behind her.

It is a fool's errand, she thought. *But better a fool than a victim.*

In truth, she did not know whether La'Dir had spoken falsehoods or not. Viniri was a man you listened to, but did not trust. She did not know if the man called Corpse was still alive, or if the other guards had fallen and joined some infernal mutiny. Kirka did not think about these things. She followed directions, because doing so gave her many opportunities to kill. And killing was the finest pleasure she had ever known.

The clank of armor and hissing of cats created a cacophonous symphony. It would've been wiser to come in on foot, quietly, with one good soldier, than fifty of these club-footed beasts. Ultimately, it was not her decision to make.

"Captain!" shouted one man.

A plume of black smoke billowed from the treeline. "Follow it," she said. "Spread out. I want a distance of four men between each of you. We will find our Corpse."

They did as she said. Somewhere, in the distance, she heard a scream.

* * *

Jessa's eyes were closed. He bowed his head.

The magic did not come so easily here, even with the trade of time.

Not when he had to fight so hard to keep his mind right. Visions intruded, emanating from the breathing, fleshy thing, but he could push them out.

The tower was playing a game with him, he knew. It only had to wait him out. It only had to be patient and Jessa would either succumb to its powers, or the cost of his own sorcery would lead him to certain doom.

Jessa held out a palm, as if to feel the red-tinged air. It permeated his body now. It was a sickness he would never be rid of.

This was a game of wills.

He was sent for a reason.

Jessa reached within himself and conjured what he could. Minutes, hours, years—a lifetime—rested within his will. Time was a weapon potent enough to demolish all things.

He pushed the visions from his head and focused. The red light touched his skin, spreading warmth like a mother's salve. He could not hear the footsteps behind him.

* * *

Corpse saw violent visions of nothing. They lied beyond his ability to comprehend. One blade stabbed him, then another, and another. Each bit into him and in a daze he could do nothing but fall to the earth, his mouth open in agony. Crumbs of dirt filled his mouth, caked his beard, but the pain was such that he could do nothing and see nothing.

If this was the end, it was more terrible than even he could conceive. The end was long, slow, bloody, and painful. It seeped out of him an ounce at a time, as angry hellions prodded the life from his body.

Until, however, the prodding stopped.

Blades clashed somewhere in the distance.

He wished to die. If only for the pain to end. *Only a little longer,* he reasoned. *And finally my body will be reclaimed. This tumor shall return to the earth.*

Men screamed. Boots scurried through brush. Great riding cats crushed skulls between their strong jaws.

Corpse barely understood any of this. Bodies fell beside him. Heads rolled. Blood sprayed. As the blackness crept through his body, he realized one thing before his mind went blank: *finally, I am dead.*

* * *

THE PATH HOME was not a treacherous one. He simply went the way he came—seeing firsthand the swath of destruction he and his ilk from the Malwoods had caused. There was no treachery because there were no people. Their lights had been snuffed and in their place was ruin. Corpse felt a wave of sadness as he passed these remains. The smell of fire lingered. Nights ago, these regrets were only seedlings. But how they had grown.

Yes, *he decided.* It is best if I die.

Every time he witnessed the deja vu of a blood-stained street though, he saw the man holding his daughter's lifeless corpse, begging to live with a lifetime of that agony, rather than nothing at all. A wound opened in Corpse's heart. But he pressed on.

It was time to go.

He reached the Malwoods at the end of his sixth night of travel and when he stood before those towering trees that pierced the sky with their tips, he felt his muscles go slack. He fell to the earth, not out of exhaustion, but a primal desire to join with it, to end his own curse rather than be forced to solve his own mind.

It was only an hour's walk from the edge of the Malwoods to Corpse's own unnamed village—a place of dirt holes and desperate, nervous people praying for suicidal strength. These were lonely woods, perhaps by design. Which was why Corpse was surprised to see the woman.

She was from the village. Dressed as a priest, like him.

"You can't go any further," she said.

"Why are you dressed like that?"

"Because it is what I am."

"You weren't fit for the priesthood. You've deserted." He remembered it when he was a child. She was older than him, but had struck out on her own during his infancy. When she returned, he was told to treat her as a pariah. A broken animal too stupid to die. Therin was conniving, unstable—but her treatment upon return rendered her cruel.

"And now so have you," she said, a wicked grin on her lips.

Corpse eyed the woman carefully. She held a blade. From the look of it, freshly sharpened.

"I know what I've done," he said. "It is why I've returned home. I've seen horrible things and I am ready to pass on. Please move out of my way and I will find my grave and you will not have to worry about me any longer." He started forward.

"Not so fast," said Therin. "General Loss sent word through our seer that you'd likely be returning. Our council had a meeting as soon as word came."

"And?"

Therin raised her blade. "I saw an opportunity."

"Do tell."

"I volunteered to battle you, if you insist upon it. And if I lose, I get what I've always wanted. And if I win, I make my time that much more tolerable."

"Status."

"Yes, status."

Those with status were afforded more pleasures, they were more easily able to distract themselves from the great maw that would swallow them.

"I don't wish to fight you."

"Then you can leave," said Therin. "But you can't die here. Find yourself a lonely gulch and rot far away from us."

"I have a grave," he said.

"It's been filled."

"What?"

"Our elders are taking this very seriously."

"For desertion? I—" Corpse cut himself off.

"Aye," said Therin. "Perhaps you're getting it worse than others. But to be fair, you were much too lauded before anyway."

"And if I refuse to leave my home?"

"I will kill you."

"You can't."

"I'm more than capable," she said. "And as I said, I have nothing to lose, and everything to gain." Her fingers wrapped tightly around her hilt. "It'd be an honor to test myself against your blade, O Warrior Corpse. The Feller of Men. The Black Blade of Eternal Absence. Our Most Treasured Priest of Death. Aye, I've heard of your triumphs. I've felt the sweet lies of your victories, the momentary glory of the transference of pain. But like all distractions, they last as long as a story, and no longer. It'd be my pleasure to end your story today, Corpse. You only need take one step forward."

Rage coursed through his veins. "Arrogant. A grown child. And I'm forced to endure your tantrum? Stand aside or I will give you a fate worse than death."

She licked her lips. "If you want to fight, you need only to step forward. One tiny step, Corpse. No more talk."

Corpse drew his sword. "So be it. Stand aside."

Therin charged, the point of her blade pointed dead at his heart, her teeth bared. Corpse parried the attack, the clang of metal on metal resonating through the woods. But Therin was prepared. Her blade dipped under his and slashed forward, once again aimed at the center of his chest, as if she meant to carve out his heart.

Corpse retreated, pivoted to the side, and let Therin pass him. She stumbled toward a bed of pine needles, before righting herself and spinning, swinging her blade in a wide arc that nearly sliced the skin of her opponent's cheek.

She was more skilled than he thought. Sloppy, yes. But dangerous. Clearly, her mind was quick.

Corpse had not attacked yet, as it was his preference to respond to his opponent. To feel out their particular brand of violence as if it were a dance. They would lead, and he would follow. And when he learned the steps, he could turn them against him.

Therin recovered from her swing and Corpse feinted to her hand—a quick slash, short and purposeful to draw out a reaction. She held steady.

Good, *thought Corpse.* She's no beginner. Perhaps her pariahship had been put to use.

But it would only take one mistake.

When both their breathing ran hot and fire burned within them, Therin grew desperate, bored, impatient; she raised her blade above her head and Corpse saw his opportunity present itself. With a firm hand and strong arm, he sliced his blade up, into the V that her arms made around the sword's pommel, hammering its bottom, sending it flying out of Therin's hands, where Corpse plucked it from the air.

When she saw the two blades in Corpse's hands, she shut her eyes tight, bracing herself for the horrific nothingness.

But it did not come.

Corpse threw her sword aside. "You counted on death or victory. But you were wrong. There are worse ways to live." His voice was a whisper. "I will not kill you. Instead, I'll leave you wishing I did." With a single motion of his wrist, he cut deep into her arm. Blood seeped out of the wound, traveling down her limb in a crimson bead. Her eyes were fiery and wet, lit with hate. "You will continue to be a pariah," he said. "And I will leave."

Corpse left silently, his heart buried in the grave that his people denied him. He did not know where he would go.

* * *

IN THE DRUNKEN PROPHET, Garrt and Mirth spoke in Therin's empty room.

"Where could she have gone?" he asked.

"I can think of only one place."

Garrt sat on the bed. "Mirth, a large portion of the Count's guards are in the woods. There are too many of them. We will be among the dead."

"I already am," said Mirth. "I'm old, Garrt."

"Yes? And you enjoy being alive do you not?"

Mirth held her chin to her clavicle, unmoving. "I do," she said. She forced a pained smile. "But it's not as easy as that."

Garrt took her hand in his own. "So, let's make it easy,

Mirth. What is it that you want? What is so important about this Corpse fellow? Was he such a powerful lover?"

Mirth laughed and Garrt playfully pushed her.

"No," she said. "He was quite unpracticed."

"Then, what is it about him?"

Mirth said, "I don't speak of it much, but I think a lot about the girl I saved from death."

"Therin."

"Yes, or rather, the child she was. Not the woman she'd become. I've gotten letters from her for years. I see her words and my heart beats and I feel like I'm receiving a note from my own child. Isn't that silly? I spent three days with her eating food and watching plays and now I think I'm her mother. I'm every bit of the entitled bitch Viniri believes me to be."

"You're a person who cares about other people," said Garrt. "It's a state of being unworthy of shame."

"I hate her letters," said Mirth.

"Oh?"

"I hate them."

"How so?"

Mirth hung her head even lower, gentle rhythms of sorrow rocked her body. "They are not good letters. I have seen the real Therin. The real Therin is not a good person. She does not care for others. She's an addict for resentment and violence. The tales she tells me in her letters keep me awake at night. I have nightmares."

"And yet she still writes to you."

"I thought I had a child all this time, Garrt. But I think I've really had a parasite."

"Some would say they're the same thing."

"I've been made a fool," she said. "Therin will try to kill

Corpse. She will not cease looking for him until his head is strung, dangling on her back."

Garrt thought for a moment. "We could go in after her, could we not? We could stop her?"

"Yes, perhaps." She stared up from the floor and light glinted within her wet eyes. "But we're not warriors, Garrt. We're innkeepers."

"We're more than that, Mirth," he said. "We're people that care for other people."

Mirth wrapped an arm around him, pulling him close. "I am lucky to call you a friend."

"Aye," he said. "I reckon you are."

* * *

Kirka Rust's blade slid in and out of bodies with the speed of a serpent's tongue. She favored a thin blade with a needle-like point, taking pride in finding new and effective angles to punch her tip between plates of armor into the most essential organs. In training, she was jailed briefly for killing classmates. One or two was an acceptable quota—some would even say that having none die by your blade was worse than one or two. But Kirka had killed *every* one of her fencing partners. At ten, they took her away to a dark cell for a week, allowing her to return as an instructor—armed only with a wooden blade.

When her soldiers saw the red-eyed deserters, she was glad to once again have steel in her hand.

There were only a few of them. They were busy stabbing a body—one of several—covered in blood. She was not sure if they were her own men, Corpse, or simple vagrants.

"Kill them all!" she shouted. Her men screamed their war cries and chased down the small squadron of mad-eyed killers. She dismounted her cat and came to meet a young feral girl with a spear so caked in blood that she thought for a moment it was made of bone.

Kirka's blade met her brain in seconds.

The girl fell.

She fenced through their defenses easily. La'Dir was a coward, she decided. The man was not fit for this job, was not able to fulfill a simple duty to Dross Toll. Surely, these beings were aided by magic, but they were not powerful. They moved erratically. Distracted, yet rabid.

Their heads were taken. Their bones were smashed. The battle raged.

Kirka stood back to watch the last of them fall. By her count, they had lost less than three men.

It was a good day, a day that would become one story in the legend of her life.

"Search the bodies for our Corpse," she said with a laugh. "Tonight we will feast and be drunk."

The men cheered.

* * *

THE MAN PRAYING before the tower was rendered into a bloody pulp.

Therin licked the blood he gave her from her lips.

A zealot, she thought.

The tower stood in front of her. As with all life, she felt despair for it.

She closed her eyes. *Could it be killed? Could it be saved?*

She did not know.

But it *reached* out to her. It touched her.

Therin had not found Corpse. But perhaps she had found something better.

Words slithered in through her ears. "*What do you fear most?*"

She needn't answer. The breathing tower *knew*.

Visions flashed inside of her skull. Archaic languages lapped at her ears.

She welcomed all of it.

19
AN ARMY GROWS

Kirka placed her thin blade against her ribcage. She pressed it as she took a deep breath, feeling the point break skin and pierce her still beating heart. It continued uninterrupted.

This was it.

Her memories and pride were replaced.

It only took one bite.

And one bite turned into more. The lot of them sat in the underbrush and mourned together, howling like wide-mouthed jackals as their minds and bodies transformed.

The red glow persisted.

New orders came in the form of strange and unforgettable whispers.

"*Go forth*," it whispered. "*And spread.*"

* * *

"*Am I to join the battle?*"

"*No," said the tower. "Walk, child. And keep walking.*"

20

IN THE DARK OF THE NIGHT, A HOPELESS CORPSE LIES

THE HALLS of Castle Viniri were like that of a crypt. It had only been six hours, but the guards had not yet returned. Viniri jumped at every sound, drumming his hands on his knees as he listened for footsteps.

But there were no footsteps, there was nothing. The guards were gone, the few servants that remained stood outside, dressed in ill-fitting armor, pretending to be killers. The rest worked in the kitchen, somewhere so deep in Viniri's home that he could barely remember how to get there.

The quietness of the castle disturbed him greatly, although he did his best not to show it, even to himself. Dross Toll was a place of life, but now it seemed dead.

He reflected quietly in his private quarters, watching a bowl of hot soup grow cold. Outside, a slate gray sky went on forever. He wondered if the people below him, the commoners that toiled on his land, felt this same sense of ennui today. Or, perhaps, they found salvation in their Martyr.

The woman with two heads stared back at him from a

tapestry hanging on his wall. He averted his eyes from her. His current present was so anxiety inducing, he had to wonder what past and future mated to birth it.

Viniri stood up and made his way into the halls of his castle. He felt like a ghost. Even though he was born in its heart, even though he had lived in Dross Toll his entire life, the castle did not feel like his own. It had been in his family for a thousand years, and yet: he did not think anyone could ever truly own it. Viniri was only the latest borrower, a fact that bothered him to no end.

In his time on earth, he did his best to distract himself from his own fears. Viniri was wealthier now than even his father, much wealthier than anyone in Dross Toll. This wealth, the grandeur he lived in, would be his legacy. But perhaps the people he ruled over would remember him too. He was the whip that made their skin tough with scars.

In the lonely halls of his great castle, he thought toughness was as good a legacy as any.

He climbed the steps of a spire to a private library that he once considered the strategic heart of Dross Toll. Of course, there had never been invaders. There had never been wars except for the ones he waged on his own people. Over time, the boy excited for war became a man starved for it. But the spire's library, with its bird's eye view of the city and its surroundings, were a frequent place for the Count to languish. Even without battle, it was the only place in the castle that felt like *his*.

He leaned on the stone window sill. Somewhere, far off in the distance, he heard thunder. Rain drizzled in rivulets down the window pane. Count Viniri sighed. Perhaps he would sleep.

* * *

"Sire."

When Viniri opened his eyes, only an hour had passed. The servant had his hands out, as if he were unsure whether to touch his master or not. When the Count's eyes flicked open, he immediately slapped them to his side.

"What is it?" asked the Count, his voice thick with uneasy boredom.

"There's been a fire."

"Where?"

The servant pointed out the window. "There, sire."

Viniri stood from his sofa. Thick black smoke trailed from the outer edge of Dross Toll. "Some idiot stuffed his furnace full of pitch, perhaps?"

The servant shrugged. He made no attempt at analysis. "I cannot say, sire," he said.

The Count squinted. Vaguely, he saw a shape. He could not quite make it out, but it filled him with cold dread.

He motioned to the servant. "Bring me my looking glass." The servant took four strides to Viniri's desk (which would've been only two from the Count himself) and handed him the collapsible scope. Viniri lengthened it and placed his eye to the glass circle. He blinked.

In the round glass of the looking glass, he saw his own guards, all of them—the ones he had lost and the ones he had sent to bring those lost back—burning huts down with torches, beheading peasants with uncommon glee.

"Fuck the Martyr," he said.

The servant, unnerved, took several steps back to the door.

"How many guards do we have inside the castle right now?"

"Twenty, maybe," said the servant. "Should I send for them to quell the threat?"

"What? No. Of course not. Keep them on guard in the castle."

The servant faltered for only a moment, before giving a short "Yes, sire," and scrambling down the steps.

Viniri nervously played with his jewelry as he watched the flames rise.

* * *

Panic.

Immediate panic.

Mirth and Garrt knew something was wrong before they even smelled the smoke. People were running, screaming. Many of them fled into the serpentine church and just as many of them were trampled on the way there.

Mirth and Garrt held each other in an alley between a butcher and a blacksmith. Throngs of people rushed past them.

"We have to get to the woods," said Mirth.

"There's no way," said Garrt. "There's no way in hell we're getting anywhere."

A child tripped in front of them, just an arm's reach from their hiding spot. Mirth offered a hand to the boy, kneeling down.

The boy did not see her though, he was too busy covering his head from the trampling feet.

Mirth said, "Come here, let me help you. You can be safe with us," but the boy couldn't hear. Only the droves of smashing footsteps and the rage of fire and the death rattles of the newly executed.

Garrt shook his head. He saw the future before Mirth could fully grasp it.

The boy twisted onto his stomach to crawl to safety. His

little dirty hands clawed for purchase on the earth, but each time he reached they were stamped on. He yelped, cried. Garrt said, "Look away," but no one could hear him.

The boy whined as his hands were bloodied, his back broken. A heavy step sent his head into the ground, blood and spit made a thick strand connecting his mouth to the earth. A tooth came out. The boy cried and spat another. As he did, another foot slammed down on his spine, and another, and another. He squirmed impotently like a salted slug as Mirth looked on in horror.

But the bodies would not stop coming. As the boy was smashed into the earth further and further, they seemed to think of him less and less. His blood mixed with the mud and it was no longer red, but brown. Bare feet pounded the mewling child deeper and deeper, flatter and flatter was his body. Mirth shook her head in revulsion but even she had to admit it was easier to look at him like this.

Garrt took her by the shoulder. "Back here," he whispered. "We can hide back here, until the madness stops."

Black smoke hung in the air. Somewhere, Mirth heard the sound of women wailing, of metal clashing. Dross Toll was at war.

She followed Garrt to the back entrance of a shop, where he broke the door off its hinges. Inside the blacksmith's workshop, the roar of battle dampened.

Garrt sat in a corner and Mirth sat beside him.

"I wonder what's happened to the inn," she said absently.

"Nobody's coming out of this unscathed," he said. "Not even you."

"I suppose not."

"Are you alright?"

"Yes. I think so."

They clasped each other's hands in the dark, musty storage room and listened.

The screams never stopped.

Gray light peered in between the slats of the ceiling, water droplets fell with the light.

"It's raining," said Garrt. "That'll help with the fires. Maybe the inn is safe."

Mirth shook her head. "It doesn't matter now."

"No, I suppose it doesn't."

They stayed there, cold seeping into their bones, as that gray light dimmed to indigo, and finally to black with the occasional brilliant flicker of orange. At one point, Mirth tried to keep track of the state of Dross Toll by the sound of the stampede—but that soon faded away. Same with the screams. She did not hear people anymore—which was worse than hearing them die.

"I'm going to take a look," said Garrt.

"Quickly," she said. "Don't linger."

He grabbed a small knife from a table and held it with the blade pointed down as he cracked open the door and stared out into the inky black. After a moment, he stuck a foot outside, then soon his whole body disappeared out the door.

Mirth held her breath.

"Garrt," she hissed.

Dross Toll sounded like a smothered infant.

Footsteps, on the ceiling.

Mirth found a hammer and held it close to her chest. "Garrt," she said again.

From the roof: "It's me," he said quietly. "They've made their way into the city center. They're heading to the castle."

"And what of…?" She couldn't bear to say it. *What of the people? The children? The homes? Who was attacking us?*

Grimly, he said, "Perhaps, whether it is for our Corpse or not, it would be best to make our way into the forest."

When he came down from the roof, his face was pale. Mirth saw how old he was in that instant, or rather: how much he aged.

"It's bad?"

"Yes."

She hugged him tight, and after, they steeled themselves to see the remains of which they only caught a glimpse. In the street: trampled bodies with broken bones, rendered to nothing more than pulp. Fires tore through homes and shops. The scent that hung in the air was that of iron and smoke.

Mirth and Garrt averted their gaze from the bodies as they ran through the streets toward the trees, humming softly to themselves to drown out the bloody burial rites of Dross Toll.

21

THE EMBERS OF DROSS TOLL

The world was full of people who did not want to die.

If he were searching for something to blame—that'd be it.

Viniri's hands shook as he holed himself up in his tower. "I need the staircase lined with men. Guards, servants, cooks, whoever the fuck we have on hand. Get them up here, give them a spear."

The church had caught fire; a burning 's' slashed across the city. Viniri turned from the window, shaking his head. But he couldn't look away for long. The destruction was magnetic.

The Count searched into the dark wells of his mind for an ancient curse, a bit of tidy sorcery to save his kingdom.

But Drosleté was designed as such that large displays of power demanded a great debt. Viniri, in a natural state, had only thirty more years of good life left. An act of magic large enough to destroy this army and quell Dross Toll's fires would be more time than he had to spend.

In the shadow of his castle, the invaders' numbers had grown. They had converted peasants, farmers, layabouts. He could see them teeming in the shadows, surrounding the home that was not his home.

Why couldn't the man have just died? Then none of this would have happened.

Viniri shook his head. Alas, the world was full of people who did not want to die.

* * *

SOMEWHERE, a martyr laughed.

22

THE MARTYR AND
THE GRAVE DIGGER

RIDING cats lounged in the forest's underbrush, tearing strips of flesh from dismembered bodies. Garrt held a lantern up to see their muzzles glistening with blood.

Even alone, they whispered.

"We might never find him," said Mirth. "How are we to find him in this mess?"

Garrt said, "He's likely dead. We should consider leaving this place far behind."

Mirth did not want to admit it, but it was true. Their safety was not assured if they stayed near the city. Still, she could not let go of the memory of the tender man that made love to her—a sweeter reflection of Therin. And if half the tales she'd heard of his prowess in battle were true, then he'd likely be the only one that could save them.

"We should search for him all the same," she said.

"Aye."

The forest floor was littered with body parts. Mirth had to watch her step so as not to slip on an unattached finger or foot.

It did not take long. Even in the dark of the night, lit

only by a lantern, Corpse stood out from the piles of dead. He was curled into a ball, pale as the underbelly of a fish.

Mirth touched him. "He's cold."

"Dead, I reckon."

Garrt kneeled, shining the light on the man fully. Corpse's beard was thick with earth and innards. His eyes were closed in peaceful reconciliation. Mirth joined him, stroking the bristles atop his head.

She smiled, slightly. A pained thing that she was glad Garrt could not see. "He *does* look at peace."

"His kind... they wait all their lives for this, don't they?"

"They do, in their way."

Garrt nodded, only to repeat. "He looks at peace."

She felt for his pulse. "He's gone. That's it. He's gone." The words came suddenly, sputtering out from her lips. "The poor boy," she said. "The poor man."

Garrt averted his gaze. "There is a lot in a name," he said. His eyes flickered black in the shadows of the lantern. "Mirth. You were named as is the custom of those in Dross Toll. Your father embraced his status, he gave you a happy name. There are a number of those within our city, are there not? Cunning the fishmonger, Laughter the woodchopper... It's an old tradition across the land." He gestured to the body in front of him. "Corpse too. His people, in the Malwoods, follow the same convention. They name their children for what they wish them to be. Mirthful, funny, kind, or... a corpse."

"Another reason for Therin's resentment, I suppose. She was not born into the Malwoods, but adopted. I doubt she knows the meaning of her name."

"Do you know what my name means though, Mirth? I don't think you've ever asked."

She shook her head, catching only the faintest whiff of

where her friend was taking her. "I don't, *Garrt*," she said, savoring his name on her tongue.

"Garrt is a name my parents gave me. It comes from the old language, the one we buried."

"I knew your name was strange, but I did not realize—" Mirth felt ashamed at the realization. They had been friends for a lifetime, and yet, there was more to learn. She shook her head. "I've never seen you use magic."

"I never have," he said. "But it is within my blood. I am not fluent in the language, unlike others. My parents taught me some but found the risk to be too great and quietly assimilated. It is our kind, I suppose," he said bashfully. "We disappear into the background, my people —a long line of peasants who traded time to build homes, to find food, and ultimately, to escape the clutches of a lifelong despair. Still, we have our traditions. Garrt was a name bestowed upon me, symbolic of my parents wishes—it comes from *g'arrtha*. It means rebirth." His expression became solemn. "I didn't think it mattered," he said.

She touched his shoulder. "Friend, what do you mean to do?"

Garrt was younger than her, but only by a decade. She had babysat him as he ran naked through the streets. They had grown up together, became friends as adults; fucked, loved, and shared many meals. In the light of the lantern, slashes of black cut his face. He said, "Bring back our Corpse."

"I always thought of you as a child," Mirth said. "I suppose you're not but you don't have to do this. I know that's what I'm supposed to say, but it's not *just* something I'm supposed to say. It's something I mean. Corpse is dead. We can leave and never come back, our old bones will break and turn to dust inside our bodies." She laughed at that, swallowing. "But we can just go."

Garrt touched the body of the man named Corpse. "He's really just a boy, isn't he?"

"Aye," said Mirth. "But—"

Garrt raised a hand. "Please, Mirth. Hear me out. I have not traveled like you. I have not read like you."

"I'm a child of privilege, Garrt."

"Let me finish. My family is old. They're buried under the earth of Dross Toll. How many generations? A hundred? More?" He placed his hand over his heart. "They are the dirt beneath our feet. They are the soil that grows crops. They are my past, I am their present, and I don't have children, Mirth. The line ends with me. I have the chance to give Dross Toll its future."

"Beneath my friend hides a patriot," she said with a half-smile.

"The man here is just a boy. He doesn't know it yet, and he might not ever find out, but he has a life worth living. He can do great things. His melancholy does not consume him, not entirely. If it had, he would not have made love with you. He would not have defended a stranger in the street. He would not have fought valiantly in this merciless forest."

"Garrt, please. He's dead. They killed him."

"Then, he shall learn from his mistakes."

Mirth stared into her old friend's eyes, reaching out to touch his cheek. "You're not a sorcerer, Garrt."

"No, I'm not. But I'm a barkeep with a good memory. I will do my best."

"And what is it that you remember?"

"The story of the Two-Headed Martyr. The other half of the tale, the apocryphal lessons. The ones only written in the old language."

Mirth sighed. She'd heard only vague retellings, hints of the second half of the story. It was there, of course, whispered amongst the commoners of Dross Toll. Sometimes, a priest would make mention of it in church, but only as a vague allusion or joke. A lost chapter.

Garrt said, "I grew up with it. Those who study the old language do. The story is longer there, and cannot be spoken aloud in its true words or else risk catastrophe. We all know the beginning, our Martyr can see the past and future, each with one head, and between them, they convene and create the present. And then, of course, the Lord kills her. This is the extent of the tale for most of us— and it is a tale simply of how time manifests. It provides hope for us poor folk."

"And a means for the rich folk to control the poor folk."

"Yes. But in the old language, there is a second part to the story."

Mirth laid her head on Corpse's cold body, stretching herself out on the forest floor. She blinked away a tear and said, "Make love to me, friend. And then tell me. One last time, will you?"

Garrt kissed her on the lips, softly. He placed the lantern beside her. "Of course," he said.

* * *

WHEN THEY FINISHED, they were nude and alone except for the dead man from the Malwoods beneath their heads.

Their hands intertwined as they stared up at the stars through the needles of pine.

"Why didn't we ever have children?"

"We didn't want any."

"Yes, but what about now? If you had children, would you still want to give your life?"

"I hope so," he said. "But I don't know."

She nuzzled her head into his neck. "Tell me your story. The other half of the Martyr's tale."

"Okay," he whispered. The destruction of Dross Toll was far away from them, in another place, another life. They held each other close and wallowed in the warmth of that reality for a little longer. Garrt said, "After the Martyr was killed, as the old tale goes, a grave digger was forced to bury her. Except, he was a common man and had little use for the past or future. He was concerned with what was at hand. He was a man who could barely feed his family. What care did he have for another life? And worse, he was insulted. Because there he was, alone in the graveyard, while the rest of the city was mourning the death of their martyr. The grave digger worked for the lord and as such, his loyalties bent to who gave him gold. So, he was already disgusted by the chaos this martyr had caused. Whilst digging her grave, he couldn't stop staring at her. He began to think of her less as a woman and more as a freak. A being that defied the natural order. It turned his stomach to see her. He made it no more than three feet before nausea overtook him and he swore to himself that he could not continue. Of course, this is why the story is not told often, why it has been buried by time, relegated to the annals of folktales. No one wishes their martyr to be seen as a freak and disposed of unceremoniously in a shallow grave. But it is worse still. The grave digger found her two dead heads with four dead open eyes to be so revolting, he decided he could not stand to see her as she was anymore. So, he dragged her heavy body from the cart and threw her into the grave.

"He thought, at first, that the black of the grave would cover her faces. And for a moment they did. Surely now, he could end the night early. He would fill in the grave and she would rot there unseen, with no marker to give her any sense of import. The Lord had demanded she be nothing but dirt and the grave digger was happy to aid in this command.

"Only then, the moon came out behind him and suddenly those four eyes reflected light like newly polished silver coins. The Martyr's heads faced each other, as if they were whispering secrets in the shadows of their own grave. The grave digger shuddered. He asked himself if what they said about this grotesque creature was true. Did she weave the present out of strands of the past and future? Was his Lord—who kept him so poor, but not as poor as others—truly a mad tyrant? He could not say. But as he looked into the Two-Headed Martyr's eyes, suspicions and unsettlement lurked within his brain. *I will end this!* he told himself, *once and for all!*

"He placed the blade of the shovel on one of the Martyr's necks and then brought his foot down. The head came off without much resistance. He did the other next. Then, with the metal edge of the shovel, he turned them to face toward the earth. Now that the Martyr was no longer staring at him, he felt he could continue filling in her grave. So, he did just that."

Garrt took a deep breath, then kissed Mirth on the forehead. He said, "But, that's not the end of the story, of course. After the grave digger beheaded the Martyr and turned her heads to the earth, he filled in her unmarked plot and went on his merry way. For the next week, he dug graves as zealots were executed. These zealots were the followers of the Martyr, those that could not accept her death, and those very same that we stand on the shoulders of now. The Lord had them flayed alive then buried as they mewled and whimpered. Some say you can still hear their cries from under the earth in the old cemetery."

"I've heard that part of the story," said Mirth quietly. "My father told me not to go there at night. Especially in the winter. He said the spirits can remember the cold hitting their raw nerves."

"Yes, I've heard them." He paused for a moment, shook his head. "Many old stories circle about like that. They're retold and recontextualized. They're given new life in new surroundings. Our grave digger, though, was the first to tell this story. He heard them in their graves, alive—barely—as he piled dirt over their bodies. The raspy gasps of their skinless bodies, begging to be released from life, followed him into his nightmares. When he saw those things, he also saw four glowing eyes in the blackest shadows of his dreams. Alone, in the dark of his hut, he woke in a cold sweat, dreading the awfulness of his work, the continuing horror he felt every day. And in a moment of resolve, he said aloud: *no more.*

"Back in those days, we weren't as disconnected from the old language. It was still in use. Now, it is maintained by the wealthy and privileged, for the most part, but at one time it was nothing but a way to speak—albeit a powerful means. Magic was used across Dross Toll's social classes. Even grave diggers knew a little to get by in a pinch, although the threat of losing one's life to it was a constant threat. The grave digger likely had friends and family who conjured themselves to an early grave. For him, magic was a last resort.

"After making his resolution, he went to the graveyard to dig up the Martyr. He whispered his sorrows to her, apologizing for his minuscule role in her demise, renouncing the Lord that killed her. He found her nearly as he left her, except now her heads were turned up toward the sky again. Looking into the Martyr's eyes, he pulled out a scrap of parchment from his trousers and spoke three words from the old language." Here, was where Garrt faltered, opting instead to clear his throat rather than say the words. "He said the words and it was like with each syllable the life drained from him. One word, and he felt faint. The next word brought him to his knees. The next sucked his final breath from his lungs. The last thing he saw as he fell into the grave was the Martyr's eyes opening."

"And what happened to the Martyr?" asked Mirth.

He smiled, inspecting the stars. "She's still out there, somewhere, they say. The grave digger was found in her grave, his face stricken, frozen in awe. Some say the Martyr walks today, and that is why we have the present, because those two heads won't stop spinning it. She has grown wary of humans though, and has decided to stay far away from them."

Mirth said, "The Martyr is wise."

"Indeed, she is." Garrt studied his old friend one last time and said, "I'm sorry to leave you like this, Mirth. But if I do not do it suddenly, it will not happen at all." He whispered into Corpse's ear three words: "*Te g'arrtha ka'leh.*"

And as soon as he spoke those words, his muscles went slack; his eyes closed. Warmth left him.

Corpse woke with a gasping breath.

23
IN DROSS TOLL,
AN ABOMINATION

THE FIRST HANDS he felt were Mirth's. They touched his cheek, caressed his chest. Life returned the same way it left him—a brief and violence burst. All at once, his muscles contracted, his heart leapt, his eyes opened, and air rushed into his lungs. He stared up into the night sky with terror and wonder and shock as Mirth's voice told him, again and again, that it was okay.

Words failed. When life floods into one, there are not just organs that come alive, but feelings. The last thing Corpse remembered was the peace he felt before death, and from that peace he was woken as if by an ice bath. Betrayal, rage, tenderness, love, sorrow, and shock flickered across his face in a parade under the lamplight.

"What has happened?"

Mirth motioned to Garrt, her voice choked with sobs. "My friend... my dear friend... brought you back."

"Why?"

"Martyr, what have we done?" she asked the air, her head hung low.

Corpse started up. "I saw death. I survived death," he said in a bout of panic.

"It was selfish."

"Please," he said. "Just tell me why."

The old woman told him about the attack on the village.

"The guards," he said. "They've been poisoned by the tower."

"The tower?"

"Yes," said Corpse. "In the woods, there is a tower of flesh and blood. It does things that we can not conceive. Even being near it can warp a man's mind. Those *things* are carrying out its mission."

"What mission is that?"

Corpse shrugged. "I do not know. I have never known." He paused. "Do you know what death is like?"

"No. Yes. No... That's the hardest part about getting old," she said. "When people see you, they know that your time is not infinite. They see you as if you're melting before them."

"Death is the removal of disease," he said. "It is the absence of neuroses. It is the annihilation of war or trauma or obligation." He paused, swallowing. "It is a wonderful state, Mirth. And I regret that I have left it."

"I'm sorry," she said.

"I had waited my entire life for it." His voice broke.

"There are others though. You can help them."

"There are others, yes. But in death I did not know of them. I did not exist. My vessel was content to rot. Why have I been brought back? I was at peace." Tears rolled down his cheeks.

"People in my home are being killed," she said. "Please,

understand me, there are innocent people being killed by Viniri's folly."

"Viniri," he remembered.

"Yes, there is an army in Dross Toll now. Houses are burning. Children are being murdered. They are tearing through the town and they won't stop. Not for anything." She grabbed him by the shoulder. "It was my weakness that brought you back, as much as it was Garrt's love. Blame me for your suffering, you will be my new martyr—let me suffer a lover's hatred, but spare the people who did not earn this rage as I have. You are the only one here who might be able to end this horror."

Corpse's sobs echoed through the forest. New, fresh pain flowed through his veins, emanating from his heart. "The worst part is that I am already afraid to die again. I am already scared." His hands shook. "Why? Why? *Why?*"

Mirth, helpless, said nothing.

Corpse shook his head. "Lend me your light," he said. "I will find my sword."

* * *

CORPSE SAID nothing as Mirth led him out of the woods. The old melancholy swam through his blood. Weariness returned. *This is what it is to be alive.*

And as if to aid in this realization, his first sight of Dross Toll confirmed all this. The city was indeed burning. He felt its warmth. The smell of iron mixed with smoke. In the distance, he heard the screams of citizens being cut down, dismembered, aided by the gleeful cackle of the tower's proselytizers.

"What has happened?" he asked.

"He sent more guards into the woods."

"How many?"

"Fifty."

Corpse sighed. "He has dug his own grave."

Lightning flashed in the sky and Corpse felt as if he had died again.

For the briefest of moments, he saw a silhouette.

The black edges of whatever lay in Dross Toll towered over the castle gates and it moved as a man.

Thunder. Lightning.

Houses splintered, a thousand inhuman mouths let out a horrendous scream. The giant slammed its body against the Castle's wall, shaking stone and throwing arches off its battlements.

Mirth's face twisted in horror. "I didn't know," she said.

He took a step forward, his eyes to the giant. He did not turn back to see her.

The city he had only known as a pit stop on a greater journey was all but gone. It was as she said, destroyed. Bodies were stamped into the streets, guts strewn, muddy, and trampled. Corpse was thankful that Mirth did not follow him. He was sure that he would never like to see her again.

But, seeing this devastation...

It was difficult to maintain his cold hatred. Even he, a man without a home, could see that this was home to others. Their blood coated his feet as he walked. Dipping into the shadow of a hanging awning, he eyed the treeline to see Mirth trembling in the shadows.

The earth shook beneath his feet. Swinging his blade, he turned, expecting to see a red-eyed guard, but his blade sliced through the empty air.

Nothing.

He ducked between the rubble of demolished homes

and shops to gain a view of the colossus that came to bury Dross Toll.

It was indeed a giant, perhaps 200 feet tall or more. Its shoulders came up to the castle's outer walls. Its proportions were nearly human, but unstable. Its limbs seemed to change shape, lengthening and shortening on some eldritch whim, like an oily shadow.

Corpse ran through the wreckage to get closer.

Fires raged through parts of the city and it was only because of these swirling infernos—barely contained hells that chewed and devoured the homes and people of Dross Toll—that he could see it clearly. When he did, his stomach turned. *This is not life*, he thought in disbelief. Life was a revolting thing, but this went beyond pangs of anxiety and depression, the joyless murmuring of skipped heartbeats, the threat of age, the undone seams of a body that had lived. Corpse's stomach twisted into a tight knot. This thing was an abomination.

It was not just *one* thing though, it was many. A towering mass of twisted limbs and enraged faces, a constellation of glowing red eyes peering out through the shadows of interlocked bodies and gnashing teeth. The guards had melded, meshed, and *grew* into each other; consuming the newly revived dead of Dross Toll as well. They moved as one, like a school of fish. All of Viniri's men —now joined, moving in vicious unison, adjusting their gait and demeanor as they went, tapping into some ethereal hive mind. A giant made of men.

Corpse held his sword tight. *This thing was worthy of death.*

It wrapped its hands around the castle battlements, clawing down masses of stone and dust. It roared as it did so. He saw that the mortar between the bricks of Viniri's guards were commoners. In death, they were no more than putty, a set of nerves and muscles to use and exhaust.

Watching the great Amalgam, he couldn't help but wonder if in his death he traveled to another world. Perhaps this was not the world he left, but a new one. Mirth woke him and brought him to another of her Martyr's presents.

There is no way, he thought.

But still he charged.

24
AGONY IN REBIRTH

When Viniri saw the monstrosity form in the splinters of Dross Toll, a sheet of sweat formed on his forehead. He wiped himself and thought of some old word he could mutter, one that would shave a minute or two from his life and be so cunning and pointed that it would undo the disaster in a blink.

The Count's mind went blank. He paced back and forth from one wall to the next. *Surely, there is a way out here.*

The city glowed with fiery embers. A disgusted yelp rose from his throat. Viniri shook his head. *Damned peasants, they couldn't even fight for their own land.*

But that thought led to others, and as the towering demon finally tore through the outer wall, the Count despaired.

He turned away from the window, the floor shaking beneath his feet.

A servant appeared in the doorway, "Sire—"

Viniri pushed him aside, muttering under his breath, "Out of my way, fool."

He flew on light feet down the spiral staircase, determined to make his escape.

* * *

Corpse's blade cut into the Amalgam's ankle, slicing wholly through one of the individuals that had given up their name to be sinew and flesh. The monster howled and Corpse sliced again, halving another soupy guard. Blood sprayed from the conjoined bodies, and Corpse closed his eyes lest he feel the sting of salt.

Rock and dust fell from the sky, Corpse dodged the debris through the Amalgam's feet, letting the great stones make craters in the muddy earth.

The thing stared down at him, a being of a thousand pupils, glowing a soft red in the night. Some of the bodies followed him with more eager eyes than others, these were the ones that fought him in the forest, killed him in the wet earth of Dross Toll's flank.

He swung again.

His blade bit into another guard and now the ankle was disconnected by half. The Amalgam screamed and Corpse sprung back. It was unsteady, he knew it could fall. And if it did…

Flashes of violent victory flooded his brain. To kill this thing would be to take revenge on life itself.

But the Amalgam did not fall, instead it only faltered, wobbling back and forth on unsteady legs but never losing its balance. It shifted in one direction, as if gravity would take it to earth, but then it was as if the wind pushed it right back. It bobbled like a duck in water.

The wound in its ankle palpitated with crimson light and began to reform. The gash resealed itself. Limbs connected heads, feet connected backs, faces melded with other faces. The halved and writhing bodies of the tower's minions grew in planes of twisted scar tissue and bloody afterbirth.

The thing swung a fist at Corpse, a meaty hammer the size of his body. It sailed through the air and Corpse had only a moment to right himself.

Swoosh.

Corpse rolled into a pile of rocks as the giant's hand rose up again amidst another cloud of dust. Jagged stones cut his arms, pressing deep into his muscles. A sorrowful reminder of his state. He raised himself up from the earth, letting blood flow freely down his body. He tilted his blade to the great beast and screamed.

The Amalgam's many faces—caged in its silhouetted form—smiled in unison.

* * *

THE BEAST HAD BROKEN through the battlements but had not taken the castle yet. *I wonder if it'll go away*, thought Viniri. They were the words of a child. He remembered his brief, cruel youth with a swallow of sad disgust.

Servants ran behind him.

"Wait!" he yelled. "Where are you going?"

The servants—a man and a woman—froze. The man sneered. "Fuck off."

Viniri ignored the insult, "Do you have the keys to the dungeon?"

"The dungeon?" The man stared at Viniri as if he were insane.

"Yes, the dungeon. Just the keys."

He turned to the woman. "Let's go."

The castle was empty except for the servants, and now even they were leaving.

"This was the only thing I ever had," he said. "And I never had it."

The smell of shit. Carrion. Cold. Hunger. Death in a ditch, a hundred miles away from the closest gold coin.

Count Viniri started for the dungeon.

* * *

THE BEAST CHASED HIM. Corpse ran between rows of houses, his feet burning, his legs in perfect agony. The Amalgam followed recklessly, its front limbs lengthening, thinning out the melded bodies into long running legs. It chased him on all fours like a giant hairless, faceless, dog with a hide of scar tissue.

He felt the heat on his back.

I can't defeat this thing in combat, he thought.

He turned sharply and dove between the rummage of two buildings and the thing lost its footing, dragging itself to the earth.

If I...

He spied the castle, its great gray spires threatening to spear the heavens.

The Amalgam recovered, righting itself from the wreckage of another home.

The beast had crumbled the outer wall. Corpse had the vaguest idea of escape, or at least a change in battlefield.

The Amalgam ran after him, a hundred feet of pulsating flesh. Corpse pivoted toward the great crack in the wall, reaching within himself for one last great reservoir of strength. The thing's heat kissed his back, its aura poisoned his mind with madness. Its front limb swiped at him and he could feel the flesh sliding impotently across his back, barely grazing him.

He pumped his legs harder. The thing was coming. It was right on his heels.

The stones had formed a mound in front of the crack. Corpse imagined his traipse up them, judging his stride, guessing at the power he'd need to propel himself without losing tempo.

One wrong step, and the Amalgam would swallow him with its entire body.

Corpse could not see the Amalgam dying. It was not of this earth. The fact that it could not die revolted him. And it motivated him to run fast and far. The first stone was the size of his head. He leapt onto it, then extended his right leg forward onto a jagged rock the size of a large wine barrel. Behind him, the furious heat of the Amalgam boiled his skin, but he dared not look back to see how close the beast was to his heels.

From one rock to the other, he leapt in rapid succession, scrambling up the cascade of stones to its peak.

The rocks had filled in a path through the moat. If he could slide down and leapfrog across the water, he could perhaps reach the castle door and—

The Amalgam slammed its fist into Corpse's back.

Air retreated from his lungs.

His eyes bulged from their sockets.

He sailed through the air, blissfully unconscious.

Until he hit glass.

He felt the weight of his fall in every bone.

Across his body—a thousand microscopic slivers.

His back cracked when he sat up, he shivered as the pain hit. Outside, the Amalgam roared, victorious, as it tore through the rest of the wall and crossed the moat. Corpse searched his surroundings, his head swimming. *I'm in the castle. This is a room. There is a bed. I was thrown through the air and I landed in the castle.* As he got up, he was not sure whether this had been a stroke of luck or misfortune.

He tested his limbs, did his best to shake away the pain. His sword was still in his hand, he took that as fortune.

The Amalgam loomed over the window, clawing out bricks and shaking the whole spire. It would crumble in no time. It would take but seconds.

Corpse ran out of the room, searching his mind for some idea of how to destroy the creature. *I am but a man with a sword*, he thought.

The castle shook beneath his feet as he traveled deeper into its heart.

"Castano il brita," said Viniri. A torch illuminated with liquid crimson fire. An old spell, one that cost him only a week—but what was a week at the end of his life?

He had not been down into these depths for years, not since he was a child. Back then, these black chambers held morbid fun. There were people here, and he enjoyed listening to their whines for help, teasing them. Sometimes, when there was a sick old beggar, Viniri would practice his more conservative magic. A cut here, a pinprick there. A sleeping vagrant would rush to their feet and the gilded boy would giggle from a dark corner, barely aware of the minutes gone from his life.

Now though, it was a place he seldom visited. As we grow older, we have to make choices. Pain and history sit heavy on our shoulders. For the Count, it was the same. The childish cruelties that once thrilled him became more nuanced and sadistic as he aged, but his sense of disgust for the people he kept in the dungeon only grew. He remembered a particularly horrific episode as a young teenager, witnessing a toothless old man with empty eye sockets and feeling his heart beat through his chest.

With age, magic dies too. It's a game for the young, the ones who don't realize that time is ticking away, who are impervious to fear. Yes, as he got older, these pleasures evaded him. But in the light of an old and favorite spell, he visited the closest thing he had to a friend.

"La'Dir," he said. "Good evening."

BEHIND HIM, the Amalgam's hand followed Corpse through the castle, like a child reaching into the window of a dollhouse.

It broke doorways and tumbled walls with incredible ease. Dust particles and wooden planks showered down around him. There was a great ripping sound and the roof came off.

Raindrops fell. The coolness was refreshing, revitalizing. But the black silhouette of a thousand red eyes threatened him; its body shifting again, lengthening.

No, thought Corpse. But it was exactly as he thought.

The Amalgam's limbs disappeared, vanishing into the patchwork of sinew and muscle that made up its torso. It mimicked now, in a blasphemous parallel, the great church that winded serpentine through Dross Toll. Its humanoid head became a snout with a fleshy open mouth where bones jutted out from contorted bodies to become sharp ivory teeth. It snapped at the air and then poured itself into the building, snaking toward Corpse at lightning speed.

* * *

LA'DIR HAD AGED since he'd last seen him. Bile tickled the Count's tongue. He did not like to see him like this—nude, wounds festering. He thought he showed him mercy by placing him down here. But La'Dir's appearance made him think that he showed himself mercy most of all.

"Friend," he said.

"No," said La'Dir. "No."

The Count peered through the bars, drinking his friend's pain. "I didn't mean for it to be like this."

La'Dir laughed.

The Count became the boy he once was, the boy who cowered before a powerful father. "I supposed I should say you were right."

The castle shook and a great scream pierced the stone walls.

"This is it," said La'Dir. "It's over."

"Maybe," said Viniri. "But maybe not."

"It's over, *Count*." He spat. "The Martyr will have worms crawling from your guts. You have no children. Nothing. It is over. Everything is—"

"Do you know the old language?"

La'Dir stared at him dumbfounded.

"I had an idea," he said. "It would cost me my life. But you, you are younger. You could survive. I could write the words on a slip of paper and you could say them and kill that thing out there."

La'Dir said, "You want me to die."

"You're already dead if you stay in here," he said. "I could give you freedom. Riches too. You could be the second richest in Dross Toll. You could live a perfect fifteen or twenty years…" Viniri swallowed. "Or you could die in a cell. It's your choice."

La'Dir rubbed his temples. "You tortured me."

"Of course I did. It was my pleasure."

"And now?"

"And now you are of use to me. And I am of use to you." Viniri licked his lips. "What do you say?"

La'Dir lifted his head slowly. "I have your word?"

"Yes. My word," said Viniri, a tremor escaping into his words, making them shake with the floor. "You have my word."

La'Dir nodded. "Fine then," he said gruffly. "Hand me your words."

The Count produced no quill, instead he reached into his robes and returned with a folded piece of parchment. He pushed his hands through the bars, the paper glowing red in the firelight. As La'Dir went to grab it, he yanked his hand back.

"Friend," he said. "Be careful."

* * *

Corpse ran, dodging between columns as the Amalgam's snakelike form twisted through the castle. He saw the many faces its maw contained, all of them locked into a sort of remedial workman's dread. He felt sorrow for those faces.

He slashed backward to keep the serpent at bay, but the wound in the snake's mouth closed nearly as soon as he made his cut. There would be no holding back this beast. Corpse's body was already ailing, burning from muscle ache.

Out of the corner of his eye, he spotted a hallway. His current room had a tall ceiling, one large enough that the

Amalgam could rear back. It arched its spine and opened its bloody red mouth.

Corpse ran.

The Amalgam's face punched through a stone wall. It squealed in frustration, but Corpse disappeared down the hallway, toward an old rusted metal door.

The hallway leading to the door was thin, too thin for the snake to reach into. Corpse laid his back to the door and caught his breath, watching with cold eyes as the Amalgam regained its poise and barreled toward the arch. The edges crumbled. Bricks shook. *It won't be long,* he thought. A dozen more strikes and the snake would have carved out the hallway to fit its immense girth.

Death chased him.

Breathing deep, he faced his pursuer as it beat its head bloody into the too-thin hallway opening.

If you chase, he thought, *I shall run.* And then he opened the door behind him.

25
DEATH, DECAY, AND A FITTING END

THE DOOR FLUNG OPEN, bathing Corpse in red light.

Behind him: the furious maw of otherworldly death. In front: Count Viniri's corpse, slumped in a pile of expensive robes, stripped of whatever youth and life he once had. His eye sockets were black windows into the beyond. His skin had shrunk to fit his skull. What remained of his lips were twisted into a scream of abject horror.

Corpse stalled, confused. He stared at the strange light burning from the torch. It glowed with a red, ethereal flame. A voice interrupted his thoughts.

"Who goes there?"

Corpse followed the voice, traipsing carefully over Viniri's body to the cell it originated from. He stared at the nude, wounded old man and said, "My name is Corpse."

"Of course, I know you."

"I don't know you."

"I was going to kill you, once," he said.

Corpse assumed him mad. *Who would send such a pathetic thing?*

"I looked different then," he said. "I looked very different."

"Oh."

"I killed your nemesis," he said. "You don't have to worry. Not about him at least."

Corpse pieced it together, gazing with disgust at Viniri's desiccated body. "Do you know a way out of here?"

"No. The only way out is the way you came. It's unfortunate, I think, that you are stuck here with me. I could kill you, you know. I have that power. I could kill us both and use what little of my life I have left. It could work. We would not suffer." He motioned to a scrap of paper that laid beside him. "Once last gift from our Count." He laughed wildly at that.

Corpse said, "I don't want to die."

"Many men don't want to die. And yet they do. And the people they love weep. And the people they love move on. And after, the Martyr continues her weaving."

"It would not hurt?"

"No," said the old man. "It would not."

Corpse startled at a large crash. The metal door buckled.

"It won't be long till that thing finds us, devours us. Whatever it is, we're fucked. I can kill us both. Right now. Do you want me to?"

"I already died today," he said; the words sounded like the thoughts of a child.

"If you say so. I only have so many years to spare. It would be my honor to kill you."

Corpse studied the ancient thing in the dungeon. The old man sat in a corner of his cell, his skin ravaged by age, his hair gray. He was not beautiful, not like Mirth. Corpse saw himself in the old man.

"How do I know if I am ready to die?"

"Aren't your people always ready?"

"No. Not always."

The old man shrugged. "It matters not to me."

"I've been searching for something," said Corpse. "I left my home."

"Perhaps you've been searching for this."

The metal door bent under the force of the Amalgam's savage beating. *The only thing left in life is despair*, he thought. The melancholy that swam in his blood made him feel heavy. He remembered the intense blankness of death, the brutal sorrow he felt being awoken from it. Then, he remembered Mirth. He remembered Jessa. He remembered that the world held many secrets.

But he also felt the pain inside his body, his mind. The pain he felt as a child and would continue to feel for the rest of the life. This agony followed him, it reared its head, ambushing his senses. It made good food taste like dirt. It made drunkenness feel like drowning. It brought the tip of his sword away from his enemies and to the soft flesh of his own throat. This would never end. Like time itself.

His hands fell limp. He hung his head. "Okay," he said. "Do it."

The door rocked on its hinges. Dust flew out in the red light of the dungeon.

The old man nodded slowly. "Of course," he said. "Any last words?"

Corpse shook his head. "Who would remember them?"

"Fair enough." He cleared his throat.

In the red firelight, the Amalgam's serpentine face shone crimson through the slit in the door. Corpse turned to the old man. *Is this not heroism, to look death in the face, willing?*

"*Dakari est palo.*" His words came out like the whisper of spring water bubbling through the ground.

Before Corpse's eyes, the old man aged. His wrinkles flattened and his skin hardened, his eyes rotted out of his skull. The old man withered and he was nothing.

The metal door flew off its hinges.

Corpse waited for death to take him. *Surely the old man's spell was working now, surely I will pass any minute.*

He closed his eyes tight and held his breath.

But he did not die.

And the Amalgam was now at the door, its giant head peering into the red light of the dungeon.

I did not die! Was it a trick?

Anger rushed over him.

The Amalgam opened its maw and sprung forward.

Corpse blinked.

The Amalgam hissed and recoiled. The thing rubbed its head on the floor, screeching in pain.

It had lunged toward the red flame and singed its flesh. Jessa's words circled in his brain.

"*You could dismember them fully, perhaps. Destroy their heads. Burn them, maybe. There may also be a magical means, but I do not know it.*"

Burn them.

Corpse dashed to the sorcerer's flame as the Amalgam recovered, he dipped his blade into the firelight and saw the metal shine with its burning tongues. His sword glowed with flames in the dungeon and he saw a thousand horrified eyes stare back at him as he ran toward the Amalgam, slashing his way through its serpentine head. Its bony teeth shattered in the path of his swinging blade, he followed the length of it, cutting down its center, each cut refusing to heal. And he screamed as he cut, as blood covered him from head to toe, as the mewling revenants were sliced out from their amalgamation like cancer. Corpse saw red. Madness touched his skull, but this too dissipated as his flaming blade ended the beast, one room at a time. Corpse in his rage followed the length of the thing from tip to tail, until it was nothing but burning meat from another world.

The thing's corpse smoked but it did not twitch.

In the open air of the ruined castle, raindrops fell onto Corpse's head. He dropped his sword and wept.

26

THE BLOODY REMAINS
OF DROSS TOLL

There were people here, people who hid. People who fought. People that ran for the trees, buried themselves under saplings, sank head-deep into rivers and lakes and waited and watched while the horror was fought. When the Amalgam was struck dead, they slowly staggered out of their homes. They held each other close and cried and cursed. They sang songs and lit fires and shared food. They asked themselves: "How could this happen? Why did this happen to us?"

But the question was good enough without an answer.

Corpse didn't have one, nor did he offer one. He sat back from the others who sat in the rubble of their homes and spoke of rebuilding or leaving or traipsing into the castle to find Viniri's bed to sleep like royalty, if only for a night. They did not come to Corpse, but they stared at him from afar sometimes. When they saw him, they shook the image out of their heads, as if they'd seen a ghost. Maybe that's all he was.

In the cold of the morning, Corpse thought of all he had seen in his time in Dross Toll. The blood and death, the terrible rebirth. The melancholy flowed through him, a viscous thing that poisoned his blood. And when he was ready, he took his sword, still burning, and turned to the forest, to finish Jessa's work.

"Corpse."

Mirth ran after him, as fast as her body would allow.

His mouth was a grim line.

"You're not leaving, are you?"

"I am," he said.

"Where are you going?"

"To end this," he said. "Before this sorcerer's flame dies on my blade."

Mirth said, "If you ever need anything—"

"You've given me enough," he said.

Mirth's eyes welled with tears, but she said nothing.

"I think your friend made a mistake," he said. "The old man in the dungeon tried to kill me with a spell, to take us both. I'm afraid I'm—"

Mirth grimaced. "Immortal."

"Yes." He paused.

"I'm sorry," she said. "I didn't know."

"That's always it, I think. We just don't know."

"Stay here and I can try to help you."

"You'll be dead in less than a decade and what then for me?"

"I have friends, money."

He shook his head. "I need death. Not friends or money." He turned his back to her. "I'm going to finish Jessa's business. He did not want to die and for now, that means something to me."

Corpse marched toward the forest, his blackened blade alight. He kept his face straight ahead so as to not be tempted to look back at the bloody remains of Dross Toll.

* * *

IN THE WOODS, there was something close to peace. He tried to find beauty in birds singing.

The forest was filled with idle riding cats, their muzzles caked in dried gore. Corpse whistled and a lazy feline stood on its legs and stretched. Corpse jumped atop it, feeling its hard muscles flexing underneath its coat. "Go," he said and it did. To himself he said, *Go until the red touches you, and then go further still.*

* * *

WHEN HE FELT bees buzzing in his brain, he knew he was close. "Stop," he said and the cat took its orders well. When he dismounted, he left the thing to lick its paws under an evergreen tree.

Nightmarish visions entered his head—death, destruction, fireballs that consumed the horizon. He saw faceless corpses screaming through sheets of flesh, wriggling worms crawling out from the mouths of newborns. He saw black towers that skewered the clouds, corpses the size of galaxies—rotting in blackness as scavengers picked their bones dry.

This was the future.

His body ached. Memories of weakness plagued him, memories of victory became pathetic expressions of ego. From which he came was nothing, the void. And he missed it dearly. So dearly that he could not think about it, lest he break down in tears again. He embraced his own history, a history of hopelessness.

This was the past.

The tower raged this war in his head as if it were a new

battlefield that demanded new warfare. Corpse allowed it to do its worst. The tower teased him. It puffed out its flesh and breathed and tried to claim him for its own. It showed him visions. But they were not of the now. And as long as they were not, they could be conquered.

Corpse raised his burning sword to claim the present.

27
SEEDLINGS

To see two worlds at once is no easy feat. It demands much of the body, much of the mind. Therin found herself walking oddly, struggling as she passed between ravines and raging rivers, her body a series of jerky, unproven movements.

She did not remember who she was, but she had made peace with that. She was far from Dross Toll now. She did not remember Corpse, nor Mirth, nor even the Malwoods.

It was the tower that she knew, and it was the tower that she celebrated with every step.

Smoke floated on the horizon.

She rubbed her hand, the pain speared itself to the front of her madness. Only three fingers left, but there was more of her to give.

The dagger was sharp, yet crusty with her blood. The pain subsided and she smiled. With one quick stroke, her thumb fell to the earth, a bloody trail following it.

Therin knelt down, dazed. With her good hand, she clawed out a hole to place her offering.

"Now," she said. "Grow."

ABOUT THE AUTHOR

Carson Winter is an award-winning author, punker, and raw nerve. His short fiction has appeared in over 20 publications, including Apex, Vastarien, and Chthonic Matter Quarterly. He is the author of *Soft Targets*, *The Psychographist,* and *A Spectre is Haunting Greentree*.

ACKNOWLEDGMENTS AND RECOMMENDATIONS

The Corpse Priest was an experiment. I wanted to combine the unlikely duo of sword and sorcery and Ligottian pessimism into a lean, mean horror fantasy with the structure of an action flick. Such lofty goals couldn't be met alone.

I want to thank my longtime friends and fellow writers for their support in helping bring Corpse to life, including Erik McHatton, Jolie Toomajan, Jon Olfert, TJ Price, and RSL.

Thank you to Matt Blairstone for lending me some of his Michael Moorcock books to put me into the right mindset.

And of course, thank you to P.L. McMillan and Salt Heart Press for agreeing to publish this strange novella.

Acknowledgements are grand, but I'd like to take some space here to recommend other indie horror authors to eager readers here. I can't claim this was my idea, but the lovely and talented Matt Brandenburg did it with the release of *The Dogmen Fudge Incident*—likening it to the liner notes in all of those punk records we listened to as teens—and I can't help but want to do the same. So, first, let me formally recommend all of the names above.

Secondly, let me name some others for you to add to your radar of incredible writers working within horror and the weird: Ivy Grimes, Luciano Marano, Íde Hennessy,

Emma E. Murray, Antony Frost, Patrick Barb, and D. Matthew Urban.

This is by no means exhaustive and I'm sure three months in the future I'll be kicking myself for a glaring exclusion, but the point is that horror is a rich genre that is thick with talent. Often overshadowed, indie writers treasure your readership that much more.

Finally, if you want to tell me about how much you loved (or hated) *The Corpse Priest*, or just want to put me onto the latest and greatest in horror, email me at carson.winter@gmail.com.

ALSO BY CARSON WINTER

The Psychographist

Soft Targets

A Spectre is Haunting Greentree

Portraits of Decay

SALT HEART PRESS

"Invention, it must be humbly admitted, does not consist in creating out of void but out of chaos." — Mary Shelley

We at Salt Heart Press seek the best in horror. We live for it, we crave it, we desire it — nothing gives us more pleasure than the thrills and chills found in the perfectly crafted dark tale. As such, it is our mission to seek out fresh voices in the genre, search out the new and unique, the brave and challenging. We want to be scared. We want to be haunted. And we want the same for you.

So take a look at the books we have and keep an eye out for those to come.

https://www.saltheartpress.com/

CHECK OUT THESE OTHER SPOOKY BOOKS FROM SALT HEART PRESS

What Remains When The Stars Burn Out
a horror collection by P.L. McMillan

If Only a Heart and other tales of terror
by Caleb Stephens

Confirmed Sightings: a triple cryptid creature feature
featuring Bridget D. Brave, P.L. McMillan, and Ryan Marie
Ketterer

**The Darkness Beyond The Stars: an anthology of space
horror**
edited by P.L. McMillan

Welcome To Your Body: Lessons in Evisceration
edited by Ryan Marie Ketterer

between doorways: explorations into liminal space
edited by TJ Price

Sisters of the Crimson Vine

by P.L. McMillan

Portraits of Decay

by Carson Winter